THE ITALIAN BILLIONAIRE

BRITNEY M. MILLS

CRYSTAL CANYON PRESS

To Clark, Hyrum, Hank & Millie

May you have the chance to venture into the world and discover new cultures and places.

CHAPTER 1

Gabe Alessandro stepped off his private jet and onto the runway of the small airport just outside of Cedar City, Utah. He'd been looking forward to this trip for weeks now, ever since his fraternity brother, Evan Pearson, had told him the reunion of their billionaire club of frat brothers was set to meet at his family ranch some fifty minutes away from this southern town. It meant a break from the constant grind of working at the family eyewear company, Cristallo.

He'd been traveling since four in the afternoon the day before and had to check his watch a few times to see if it had finally changed time zones from Venice, Italy. After a long stop in New York to refuel and sleep, he'd made the quick four-and-a-half-hour flight to Utah.

It had taken him some time to earn his pilot license, but as expensive as it had been, he enjoyed flying, and the flexibility couldn't be beat. The only downside was making sure he had a car waiting for him or at least a rental place nearby so he could get to where he needed to go.

Unloading his suitcase from the plane, he looked around

for signs for where to rent a car. It didn't take long, as the rental cars were set up at the end of the hangars.

"Name and identification?" the agent at the desk asked. She took Gabe's passport and started punching keys on the keyboard, looking as though she'd rather be anywhere than there. After a few minutes, she looked up and said, "What type of car would you like?"

Leaning forward on the counter, Gabe smiled wide and paused a moment to see if she'd break out of her foul mood. When she raised her eyebrows, he said, "Do you have any convertibles?"

The woman turned her attention back to the screen and then said, "We have one available. But it's yellow." She looked at him, doubt clouding her features.

"Even better. I'll take it."

With her eyebrows pinching together, she said, "You do know that it's supposed to snow tonight, right? You're sure you want to take a convertible on the roads?"

"Is that a bad thing?" Gabe tried to think of his few experiences with snow in Italy. He'd never had to think about getting a different car because of it. Most of the snow was in the northern provinces, near the ski resorts. And it had been a while since he'd visited any of those.

The woman tilted her head down and gave him a fake smile. "You might want an SUV to make sure you don't get stuck anywhere. Where is your destination?"

"Aspen Hollow."

Nodding, the woman said, "Okay, I have several crossover vehicles that I recommend for traveling there. You'll be going through some passes, and the storm is supposed to be worse later tonight." She compiled all the receipts and paperwork into a small folder and handed it to him. "Just go out this door and to the left, and you'll see signs to our lot. Just choose anything from row C. Have a nice day."

"You too." Gabe nodded and walked in the direction she'd pointed. He felt sorry for her. No one should hate their job that much. Then again, he'd been hoping this trip would rejuvenate his enthusiasm for eyewear. He'd been working so much the past few years that he'd hardly had time off to enjoy himself. At thirty, he felt as if he'd worked enough to be nearly forty already.

He made it to the row of cars in the parking garage, but none of them were what he would've picked. He'd just have to survive a week in Aspen Hollow with what he considered an elderly car. Picking the brightest red SUV they had on the lot, he loaded his suitcase and hopped in. His phone buzzed as he turned the ignition, and he smiled when he saw Evan's name.

"Pearson. I just made it to Cedar City."

"Awesome. Sam's plane just landed, and he should be at baggage claim soon. Will you give him a ride?"

"Sure thing. They said I shouldn't get a convertible, so I've got loads of room." Gabe turned around and surveyed the interior. This would be nice for a family. The thought of it brought memories of Nicoletta to the surface, and he did his best to push them away. But the ache for someone at his side and children he could cheer on in sports and other activities settled just inside his chest, reminding him that even though he had his parents and sister in his life, he was still alone.

Evan's chuckle carried through the phone, pulling him back to the present. "Yeah, we're supposed to get hit with a storm tonight, so be careful but hurry."

Gabe ended the call and watched the signs for the exit. After showing the attendant his paperwork, he pulled out of the garage and followed the signs to the commercial side of the airport.

Sam Gutierrez was another frat brother, coming from Argentina. Other than a quick conversation at their other club members' weddings, it had been quite a while since they'd spent much time together. Especially since he hadn't been able to make it to the funeral of their Delta Phi mentor, Dan Montgomery, the year before, when the club had taken a few days to be together in his memory.

Sam was waiting next to the curb with a suitcase and what looked like a laptop bag.

"You made it," Gabe said. He parked and got out of the car. Striding up to his friend, the two of them clapped each other on the back.

"Barely. I got sandwiched between two large people on the last flight, and the air broke. It was longer than I wanted; that's for sure." Sam grinned, his dark brown hair sprinkled with gray catching the dim light from the sky. Of all the frat brothers, he was the oldest by only a few months, but it had been a while since Gabe had really looked at him, and he seemed like he'd aged at least five years.

Gabe reached up and rubbed at it. "What happened to you, old man? When did you start going gray?"

"Since the year after graduation. My father was completely white by this point, so I guess I should be grateful I don't look decades older already."

After placing his luggage in the back, Gabe plugged the address for the Pearson Ranch into his phone, and they headed out.

"Are you ready to be with all the guys?" Gabe asked, watching the road as it wound around to the exit of the airport.

"Yes, I'm definitely ready for this trip. Business has been busier than ever, and I feel like I'm maxed out." Sam leaned his head back against the headrest, breathing out a deep sigh.

With a quick nod, Gabe said, "I'm feeling a little burned out myself. But you work in the energy business. I'd think you'd have plenty of that lying around." He chuckled.

Sam gave him a mock laugh. "If only that was how it worked."

Gabe didn't press for an explanation. He'd read enough in the papers about the fights over energy resources in South America, and he just hoped the stress wouldn't send his friend to the hospital for health problems like it had Sam's father...or Gabe's father, for that matter.

"I'm glad to hear it's not just me needing the break," Sam said as he stared out the window. "Now if we can just avoid all the married guys trying to set us up with women, it will be the perfect getaway."

Gabe listened to the voice on his phone giving him directions as he thought about Sam's words. As much as he wanted it to be a joke, four of their frat brothers were already settling down, and as much as Gabe told himself it wasn't a competition, part of him felt like he was going to end up last in the race.

But he didn't have time for a girlfriend right now, nor would it be practical to look for one while he was in the States. From everything he'd learned in college about American girls, as much as they talked about dating foreign guys, he'd rarely seen them actually living in Italy. He could understand that. His family was a big part of his life, one of the reasons he worked so hard, and it would be hard to live far away from them for longer than a year at a time.

"We'll stick together on that one." Gabe reached out his fist, and Sam bumped his against it. Sadness filled Gabe, but he pushed it away. He wasn't going to ruin this trip by worrying about his single status.

CHAPTER 2

Taking a long sip of her diet drink, Aubrey Pearson did her best to keep her eyes open. This was her fourth night shift in a row at the hospital, and the exhaustion was settling into her bones, making it harder to stay awake.

She'd just barely settled into her chair behind the nurse's desk when the machine beeped, notifying her of a patient's change in heart rate. Standing, she stretched and moved into the room, checking her watch on the way. Only another hour. Sixty minutes. She could make it. Then she'd have plenty of time to sleep when she went to her parents' home for the weekend. She needed the clear air and the feel of dirt on her hands.

As much as she loved Southern California, there was something about Aspen Hollow that always brought her back to a simpler time. A time when she didn't have to worry about finding a new place to rent or even how many more night shifts she'd have until she could get a break again. The hospital had lost several registered nurses in the last few months, and hiring was taking longer than expected, meaning the remaining nurses had to cover more and more shifts.

As much as she loved the idea of helping people, she wondered if there was a better way. Maybe she just needed a break from it all, a fresh perspective. What she really needed was a new list of goals, as many of the ones she'd set for her life seemed just out of reach, making her feel like a hamster in a spinning wheel, working harder to accomplish it but getting nowhere.

As she walked into the room, the heart rate dropped lower, signaling the loud beep again.

"Marsha? How are you do—" Aubrey looked at the woman's face and saw that she was asleep. Walking up, she pushed the button to silence the machine and checked all the vitals on the computer.

She turned to the woman, pulling the blood pressure cuff from the rack. Leaning in, she said, "Marsha, I'm sorry, but I'm going to have to take your vitals again." The woman barely stirred, her pregnant belly stretching away from her frame. Aubrey wrapped the cuff around her arm and waited for the machine to set up.

One of the three monitors on her belly had shifted upward, cueing the machine to beep again. Just what Aubrey had been trying to avoid. She undid the long elastic band that kept the monitor in place and began moving it around, hoping the baby hadn't gone far. With three babies in there, it was a challenge to keep tabs on their health as they tried to move in whatever sliver of room was still left inside their mother's womb.

After adding some more gel to the monitor, she placed it back on the stomach, inching it around every few seconds.

"Is everything all right?" Marsha asked, her eyes heavy and her voice soft.

Aubrey nodded, giving the woman a small smile. "Should

be. I'm looking to find Baby C. She seems like a feisty one already."

Marsha's grin widened. "She's been that way since I could feel them kick. I can always tell when she's trying to move around."

A lump formed in Aubrey's throat, and she turned to check something on the monitor. She could hear her mother's voice telling her that same thing about carrying Aubrey and her two triplet brothers, Evan and Aiden.

That had been twenty-nine years ago, but now that Evan was married to her best friend, Sadie, a deep longing filled her. She was used to having Sadie around when her friend wasn't off planning weddings, but it felt strange now, like Aubrey had become the third wheel.

She had no prospects for the future and no energy to date, knowing it would take a miracle to find a guy as great as her dad. Her parents' marriage was far from perfect, but there was something about it that Aubrey had always dreamed about. Married to her best friend, always having someone to do things with. Maybe it was just the extra time Sadie was now spending with her brother that made her nostalgic.

The monitor beeped, signaling she'd found the heartbeat. Smiling at Marsha, Aubrey said, "There she is. I think she's going to keep her brothers in line."

"I sure hope so."

"Believe it. I'm a Baby C myself, and my two brothers know to watch out."

Marsha's mouth dropped open. "You're a triplet?"

With a short nod, Aubrey said, "I am. So if you had any worries about how life was going to go, just know that time will pass and that we do grow up. My mom always said she looked at things in stages and that helped her get through the harder times. 'Two weeks, and it will be another phase,' she'd say. And we're all alive and well today."

Tears welled up in the woman's eyes. "Thank you so much. I've been on a rollercoaster of emotions lately, wondering if I could really do this or not."

Aubrey reached forward, clasping the woman's hand with her own. "You'll be a great mother to these three. You and your husband will be able to make it through this. They are going to love you. I'll be back to check on you before my shift is over." She smiled at the woman and walked out the door, that longing opening a chasm in her chest.

She'd been more emotional lately, and every little thing would cause a mound to form in her throat and her nose to burn. What about a pregnant woman had set her off this time?

As much as she didn't want to admit it, life hadn't exactly turned out how she'd planned. In all of her dreams and planning for the future as a teenager, she should've been married and had at least two kids by now. She wanted so badly to be a mother, to be able to share the same things her own mother had shared with her, but she still hadn't found her white knight.

Hanging out with Sadie for so long had seemed to ease that feeling, masking any concern that she wasn't in a serious relationship just yet. But now, she felt like she had the knowledge of beginning biology while the rest of the class somehow understood every aspect of microbiology. She hated to feel left out or behind in anything, and those kinds of thoughts just brought on the self-induced anxiety that came from thinking about what her life should be like.

She knew there was no perfect man, but she still hadn't felt that spark of connection yet, and she wasn't sure she ever would at this rate. Her mother had offered to set her up several times, but Aubrey had always refused, believing that love would happen naturally. Maybe she'd let her mom set her up once and see how it went. Anything to ease the ache in her chest.

With a wide smile, Aubrey sat down at the desk and worked on her charts. A little time with her mama would help solve things.

"You are the worst cheater there is!" Gabe said, pointing at Max across the table.

He and Sam had made it to the Pearson ranch a few hours earlier after surviving the slick roads of the canyon. The rest of the members of the International Billionaire Club had arrived before them, and these hours with them had already been some of the most relaxing time Gabe had enjoyed in recent memory.

A few of the guys had started a game of Skip-Bo an hour ago in the dining room of the family home, and out of the three games Gabe, Max, Oliver, and Roman had already played, Max had won them all and was on track to do it again.

Gabe was known as the most competitive of the ten guys in the room, but as irritated as he was about losing so many times, he was just happy to be playing with these guys instead of Evan, Tristan, and Logan.

Raising his hands in the air, Max grinned. "Cheater? I don't know what you're talking about. I'm not the dealer, so how could I be cheating?"

Gabe grunted and went back to looking at his own pile of cards still on the table. He hadn't lost this bad in quite a while. His competitive ego had reared its head, and he took a deep breath, knowing that showing his frustration over a simple game wasn't what he wanted to do tonight.

"How was your flight here?" Oliver asked, drawing a few cards from the main deck.

"Long. Nothing out of the ordinary, which is always a plus. How about you guys? When did you all get in?" Gabe leaned forward to pick up his glass of water and took a sip as he waited for Oliver to take his turn.

"Yesterday," Max said, resting both hands behind his head. "I flew in Tristan's plane with Roman and Oliver."

Gabe nodded and looked around. "I'm surprised all the wives and fiancés didn't come. Since most of you are like lovesick puppies nowadays. Whatever happened to having a girlfriend for longer than a few months?" He turned to glare at Roman.

"Isabelle is working on the wedding plans. She said she'd be able to get more done if she stayed since the wedding is coming up. You're all coming, right?"

Gabe smiled. "As long as I don't need a date, I'll be fine." That ache in his chest deepened, making it difficult to take more than a shallow breath. He laced his fingers together and placed them against the back of his head, glancing up at the ceiling. He just hoped this conversation would pass quickly and be done for the week.

"What, your mom hasn't set you up on any dates lately?" Oliver teased.

Reaching forward, Gabe took his cards and played several of them. "Of course she's tried. I think she's set me up with every girl in Venice at least once. Some of them I didn't recognize until we started talking and I realized they sounded oddly familiar."

"You can't find a nice Italian girl to settle down with?" Roman asked, eyebrow raised.

Gabe discarded an eleven to his pile and looked at Roman, waiting for him to continue the game. "It would be easier if they didn't know who I was, to be honest. And with work now, it's just gotten to the point where I don't have time to date—or even go out with friends. I almost didn't make it here because of a problem at the factory."

He'd taken less and less time off in the past two years, knowing that if he was gone too long, opportunities would be passed on to the next company who came along. The Cristallo brand name had grown exponentially since he'd taken over, and their sunglasses were flying off shelves all around the world. Backorders were typical with the sports glasses, and Gabe had already increased production by ten percent. But even with his successes, if there was another way, he'd try it. The weariness in his body told him he couldn't live like this forever.

Roman shook his head. "Please, that's everyone's excuse upfront. Jackson, Tristan, Evan. All of us thought we were too busy to date. Sometimes, things just fall into place. And others, you have to work for it." He placed a Skip-Bo card on the pile nearest him and placed his final card on top, making him the winner.

"Unlike them, I can't lose focus or the company will go under. Cristallo supports my family and the economy in Marghera, as well as the surrounding cities and towns. I can't just get distracted by a girl and jeopardize all that."

Max gave him a disbelieving look. "You don't think we all feel that way? A lot of people depend on our businesses too."

Roman nodded. "I thought the same, Gabe. But you'd be surprised at how competent the people are who you've hired or will hire in the future. Let them do their jobs, and you'll get to have a life. That's made the most difference in my life since dating Isabelle. I don't feel like I could sleep for a week every time I get home."

Gabe chewed on the side of his mouth, registering Roman's words. It was hard to find people he trusted to manage the business and allow him some time away, as his father had hired a few people to do just that and they'd nearly bankrupted the company. Keeping it in the family sounded like a great idea from the outside, but it wasn't always that easy when it was just Gabe and his sister.

But Sophia did have a way with people. Maybe once she was done with University he could convince her to help out and take some of the burden. But would he survive another two to three years?

Oliver gathered all the cards. "How about we play something else?"

They pulled out another card game, and Gabe glanced out the window as Oliver shuffled the cards. Snow had set in on the drive over and had carried on steadily until now. It was odd for him, the white fluff sticking on the ground longer than a few minutes, but was already grateful the rental car agent had convinced him to get the SUV. Some of the winding passes to get to Aspen Hollow had been covered in a thin layer of snow already, causing the car to slip a few times.

He was silent as the next game began, his mind spinning over the conversation. What other options did he have? His father's health was failing, and he could only handle the day-to-day operations for short periods of time before he was too tired to continue. But there had to be someone he could hire that wouldn't betray his trust. He made a mental note to do that first thing when he got back to Venice at the end of the week. Because even a few hours of peace made him feel energized, and he'd need that if he didn't want to burn out.

CHAPTER 4

*P*ulling into the driveway at the ranch, Aubrey parked her car, wishing the rain would stop so she wouldn't be soaked as she got out. At least the snow had turned to rain by the time she'd hit the turnoff for Aspen Hollow just after St. George.

Several cars were parked around the house, which was common when the lodge parking lot filled up. It was a bit unusual to have so many in the winter and not around a holiday, but family reunions and business retreats took place all year long.

She glanced up at the warm lights beaming through the large windows in her parents' home. That longing in her chest throbbed, making her catch a breath. This was always the place where she'd gone for refuge when she was troubled or just needing a break. But as she thought of Sadie and all the times they'd hung out around her brothers, playing tricks on them, it made her miss her best friend.

She'd always known Sadie held a torch for her brother, and she was excited to have her as a sister-in-law. It just felt as though Evan and Sadie's engagement and marriage were a catalyst to Aubrey's world spinning out of control. They'd only been back from their honeymoon a few weeks, but so much had changed in that time.

If she could find someone who would be good with kids and who would love her like her father had loved her mother for the past thirty-seven years, Aubrey could actually accomplish some of her life goals. But she wasn't naïve enough to think that a guy would solve all of her problems. She was stubborn and restless, but how to cure that, she still wasn't sure.

The rain continued to pound down on the windshield, and it wasn't letting up. Popping the trunk, Aubrey opened her door and dashed around to the back. The large drops splashed against the scrubs she'd been too tired to change out of after her shift that morning.

After hefting the suitcase up the front steps, she opened the door and walked inside. It had only been a month since she'd been home for Christmas and three weeks since they'd flown to the Bahamas for Evan and Sadie's wedding, but the pull to Aspen Hollow was tightening more and more, making her wonder whether she should look for a job closer to home. California had been great for college and most of her twenties, but it was losing its appeal. Her small hometown probably wasn't a permanent fix, but she just needed a change of some sort.

The smell of apple pie filled the air, and Aubrey wandered into the kitchen, her suitcase rolling along behind her. She heard several deep voices before she walked in, but it didn't register that there were more than the usual ones of her father and oldest brother, Darren.

Walking into the room, she stopped short as several pairs of eyes turned in her direction. Several familiar-looking males sat around the dining room table and a fold-out table, card games spread out among them. The shock of seeing them all in her parents' kitchen caused her brain to blank on their names.

"Aubrey, we didn't know you were coming home. How was the drive?" Her mother came up and gave her a hug, pulling some of the tension from Aubrey's chest and leaving comfort in its place.

"I just had to get out of there," Aubrey said, keeping her voice low. The guys from her brothers' billionaire club had all turned back to their card games or the action movie playing on the large screen in the family room. Pointing in their direction, she asked, "I didn't know these guys would be here. What's going on?"

She knew they were from all over the world, and to get all ten men together was quite the feat, especially with their demanding schedules and the fact that they'd just met up for the wedding. She just wasn't sure why they'd chosen her family ranch for this kind of thing. The middle of winter wasn't exactly a good time for team-building activities.

"Evan had planned to have it at the hotel, but a large builder show booked out most of the rooms, so he asked if they could come here. This week worked out because we didn't have any other guests coming to the ranch. They'll all be staying at the lodge." Her mother smiled at her, helping her pull off the rain jacket she'd worn from California.

Aubrey shivered and hoped her mother hadn't tossed her winter coat out. She hadn't needed it in a while. Even when she'd come for Christmas, the weather had been unseasonably warm. She leaned in and whispered, "How long will they be here?"

"A few more days, I think. They've been working on things outside when they haven't been meeting about business matters. There are a lot of good eggs in this group, Aubrey." Her mother gave her a knowing grin.

Aubrey's stomach seized up, the feeling rising up to

constrict her lungs. All the intentions she'd had to let her mother set her up flew out of her mind at that point.

"Mom, don't try to play matchmaker, especially not with these guys. They're all entitled rich men who wouldn't know how to take care of a family and a marriage." Aubrey was surprised to find her voice had risen, but she was grateful that only Aiden and her father had turned around as the others were immersed in discussion. She'd successfully avoided the men at Evan's wedding, and she planned to do the same now.

Her mother's lips pursed, and the space between her eyebrows disappeared. "You'll never

know until you give them a try."

Aubrey rolled her eyes, ready to be done with the conversation. "Okay, I'm going to take my bags up to my room. I need a shower and some sleep."

Her mother placed her hand on her shoulder as she turned away. "Sounds good, dear. Tomorrow we've got some activities planned for the guys. You should participate. It might be good for you."

Not looking back, she said, "We'll see, Mom. I'm making no promises."

Aubrey lugged her suitcase up the stairs and was grateful when she made it to the room and jumped in the shower. The warm water calmed her insides as she mulled over what her mother had said. Why did she feel like she had to help with finding Aubrey a boyfriend? It wasn't as if Aubrey could go up to someone and say, "You're single. I'm single. Let's date." She cringed just thinking about it, but that was the reality of blind dating in her limited experience.

As she rubbed her hair with the towel, her stomach growled. An internal debate began. Was it worth it to go down and have to socialize right now? She was ornery and cranky, which usually meant she should hole up and avoid people until she'd gotten some sleep.

As if in answer to her thoughts, her stomach rumbled again, and she knew she wouldn't be able to sleep well unless she filled up on something. She dressed and trudged down the stairs, wet hair bouncing along with her movement.

Avoiding eye contact with any of the guys, she moved toward the fridge, opening it to see what her mother had for leftovers. She pulled out a plastic container of chicken and popped it into the microwave and then pulled a roll from the basket on the counter and spread a thin layer of butter through the middle of it.

"Aubrey, I didn't know you were coming home." Evan grinned at her, pulling her into a tight embrace. He'd always tried to make her feel like he was the strongest guy in the world. She struggled to catch her breath, realizing that either he was getting stronger or she was getting weaker.

When he let go, her intake of breath was sharp. "I just needed some time to regroup, you know. Long night at the hospital."

Evan raised an eyebrow. "No one died, right?"

Aubrey chuckled. "No. There were no deaths on my watch. There was a woman who's pregnant with triplets. Two boys and a girl." She was grateful for the beep of the microwave to pull her away from his intense stare.

His arm slid around her shoulder, and he whispered in her ear, "You'll be fine, Aubs. You're an amazing girl, and anyone would be lucky to have you, even those brutes over there."

"I wish for once you wouldn't be able to read what I'm feeling." She laughed and wiped away a tear.

"Well, we're not identical, but we *have* spent a lot of our life together." He grinned and gave her another side hug before pulling away.

Aubrey focused on cutting her chicken into small bites. As grateful as she was for her brother's words, she'd heard them before, yet they were still a balm to her broken soul. She didn't think she'd be so worried about being alone, but it was something she'd have to remedy or get used to. Settling was not an option.

"Thanks, Evan. Is Sadie here?" She glanced around the room, hoping her friend was here to talk to.

"She's in New York right now, working with Charleigh French on the details of her wedding. I'm supposed to pick her up on Wednesday, and she'll be here for a few days before she has to fly back."

As Aubrey studied her brother's face, she realized how much he'd changed. He looked tired and like he missed his wife. She never would have thought that possible even a few months ago, but he was evidence that miracles do happen, even to prideful men.

"The time will fly, Ev. I know you miss her." She lifted her plate and moved in the direction of the island, hoping to eat her food in peace and then move upstairs for a break.

Evan moved back to the tables, sitting next to Jackson and Logan, who Aubrey remembered from college. At the other table were the Italian and German guys, but she could never remember their names. "You should come play with us when you're done eating. I could use a challenge," Evan said, grinning. "Most of the guys have given up against the Pearson luck."

Jackson punched him in the shoulder.

"I just beat you on the last hand," the Italian one said, shaking his head. His accent wasn't as thick as she expected but it took a bit more concentration to understand his words.

"I'd like to see you beat Aubrey, Gabe. She's ruthless."

Evan pointed in her direction, and the Italian one turned to look at her. He gave her a half-grin.

As much as she wanted to stick out her tongue like a five-year-old, her heart had other ideas, pounding away inside her chest. She remembered him from Evan's wedding, sitting in the row behind her. She'd glanced back once to check on Sadie's progress down the aisle, and he'd caught her attention. As attractive as he was, he came off as arrogant, and that was the last thing she needed. She'd dated plenty of men with egos.

"She is definitely that," Aiden said from the other table.

Frowning, she said, "I'm not ruthless. I just like winning."

A full grin spread over Gabe's face, and as exhausted as she was, there was something exhilarating about seeing an arrogant man humbled when she won a card game.

"I'm up for a friendly competition," he finally said, a smile spreading across his face.

Something about the amused expression on his face struck a chord within her, and she knew she wasn't going to get sleep anytime soon. That competitive streak she'd grown up with hadn't gone away as she'd gotten older, and for some reason, it roared to life.

Taking her plate with her, she sat in the empty seat beside Gabe. "Game on."

CHAPTER 5

*E*van and Aiden's sister took a seat next to Gabe, the smell of her coconut shampoo filling his nose as she moved her wet hair back over her shoulders.

"Aubrey, you remember Gabe, right? Max is right next to him." Evan pointed at each of them.

She nodded. "I remember your faces but not your names. Nice to see you both again." She gave them a small smile.

Gabe did everything he could to break his gaze away from her face. The whiteness of her teeth contrasted with her olive complexion. Her bright blue eyes stood out next to her long dark hair. If he didn't know better, she could have passed for a girl from Venice, and definitely one he'd have more interest in.

The players pushed the cards over to Gabe, and he picked them up, shuffling them together. "Do you know how to play Phase 10?" he asked Aubrey.

Her face constricted, and he felt a wave of guilt for even asking the question.

"We play a lot of games in this house, Gabe. I'm pretty sure I'll dominate no matter what game we play." She narrowed her eyes and pursed her lips in his direction, causing Gabe to grin. It had been a while since he'd met a girl with such spirit.

Gabe dispersed the cards in six piles and set the deck in the middle of the table. Max took a card and then discarded one, nodding to Roman that it was his turn.

"Is this how you thought your retreat was going to go?" Aubrey asked before adding another piece of chicken to her mouth.

"Rain, no. Coming to the ranch, yes." Evan grinned at her, picking up his card.

Jackson took his turn, and then it was Aubrey's. She reached forward and drew a card from the pile, biting her bottom lip as she decided where to put it in her hand.

"It takes you this long to decide what card to put down?" Gabe asked, smirking. His comment earned a glare from the girl, and she finally put down a card. Not the one he'd been hoping for.

He reached forward, taking his own card from the pile and switching it out. He only needed one more three to make the first set.

"So, Gabe, what is it that you do?" Aubrey looked at him with a bored expression, as if this was torture for her.

"I'm in the eyewear industry."

"Meaning?" Aubrey had stabbed her fork into the last piece of chicken on the plate and was waving it around. Gabe wondered how long it could stay on the fork.

"Meaning we work to create sunglasses and regular eyeglasses. We start with the lens materials and create the frames for them. Some of the most popular brands out there are under our company." He sat a little straighter, feeling like he'd just impressed her. When he looked at her face, he realized that she'd turned her eyes toward Max.

They kept playing, each person taking their turn. Aubrey

took a card from the pile, and Gabe saw a moment of frustration as she placed the card on the discard pile. She looked up at Max again and asked, "What do you do, Max?"

"I own supermarket chains in Germany." He barely looked up at her, focusing on his cards. Not surprising since Max had sworn off women forever. He'd been dumped or ghosted too many times to count.

"I still can't believe you're all billionaires for random industries. What are the odds that all of you would join the same fraternity?" She moved her gaze around the table, and Gabe took in a breath as she locked eyes with him.

He shrugged. "It's definitely a selling point for Hawthorne now." He chuckled, as did a lot of the guys around the table. "Mr. Montgomery was the best guy we've ever known, and everything he taught us was exactly what we needed to hear or learn."

"Is having that much money everything you hoped it would be?" she asked. Gabe watched as she sat back in her chair, folding her arms across her chest. The muscle near her jaw pulsed, and he wondered what had made her so sour.

Nodding, he said, "I think so. We can buy just about everything we want, but we can also help out our communities."

"Money doesn't buy love, though, does it?" Her chin tipped upward, and Gabe saw a flicker of pain pass across her eyes.

Raising his hands in the air, he said, "I never said it did. Some of us are okay being single for a while." He looked over at the guys across the table, all of them grinning at him. The three of them plus Tristan had all found someone they were either married or engaged to, and Gabe wasn't sure that would ever happen for him. But as the minutes ticked by sitting next to Aubrey, it got him thinking.

He'd seen her at the wedding, and he'd been intrigued, but he wasn't sure how Evan would have taken him showing interest in his sister during his wedding. Then again, he hadn't had much time to do a lot as he'd flown back to Italy an hour after the ceremony. Duty called a lot more than he'd realized, until now.

Turning back to Aubrey, he admitted to himself that he was intrigued. From the short time she'd been in the room, she'd given off several different signals, from "leave me alone" to spunky. They were qualities that both Evan and Aiden possessed, but it seemed as if those characteristics were more intense in her case.

It was her turn again, and she looked even more frustrated when she didn't get the card she wanted.

Gabe drew from the pile and smiled as the three he'd been waiting for showed up on the card. He placed the two sets on the table and discarded one card, leaving one in his hand.

Aubrey's eyes flashed again.

Gabe wiggled his eyebrows in her direction. "I'm still waiting to see these amazing card-playing skills, Miss Pearson."

She let out an annoyed sound and said, "What do I look like? A kindergarten teacher? I'm a nurse and get called a lot worse."

Evan and Aiden started laughing at that, and she gave them a look like they shouldn't be discussing whatever it was they'd thought of. She tried to keep her face neutral, but the corners of her mouth wouldn't stay down. The expression softened her eyes, and Gabe was struck again by how beautiful she was.

Roman laid down his cards to complete the level, and Aubrey shifted forward, her fingers tapping the table. He hadn't seen a woman so competitive in, well, ever. What was she like at the hospital? He pictured her tackling a runaway patient as if part of a football game.

Again it was her turn, and she had to discard without completing the sequence. Another three popped up on his turn, and Gabe put it next to the cards he'd already put down, discarding his final card. Aubrey, Evan, and Jackson were the only ones who hadn't come up with the sequence and would have to repeat the level.

Glancing at Aubrey, Gabe said, "Looks like I won that round." He gave her a half-smile and pushed his cards over to Max to shuffle and deal. He reached over to get Aubrey's cards and pass them over, but she moved them out of his reach, sitting forward even more to hand them to Max. The other guys made *ooo* sounds, and Gabe didn't know what else to do but laugh, surprised by the fire in this girl.

She reminded him of his mother and sister in some ways, although he'd never tell her that. Some things were better left unsaid, especially when he had enough on his plate without having to worry about entertaining a girl who acted as though he were an anomaly.

CHAPTER 6

After a fitful night of sleep, Aubrey woke to find the sun higher in the sky than she'd expected. Checking her phone, she found it was almost one in the afternoon. At least there was sun after the long day of rain and snow the day before. They'd stopped playing cards around midnight, and it had taken her a while to get to sleep afterward since she was still fired up about the game she'd lost to Gabe.

She'd lost more times during that game than she had in quite some time. And after every hand she had failed to complete, Gabe was there with his shoulder pushed back like a proud peacock. At least he'd stopped making comments about it after the first hand. He was a piece of work, and it didn't surprise her that he was still single. The man would be unbearable as a spouse, or even a first date for that matter.

She slid her feet down to the floor and rubbed at her eyes, wiping the sleep from them. Her hair fell into her face, and she threw it back, trying to figure out what she should do that afternoon. The fact that she didn't have to run off to work or an appointment was freeing, but it also made it harder to find the motivation to do anything.

After dressing in a pair of sweats, a t-shirt, and then a hoodie, Aubrey pulled her hair out of her face and wrapped it into a high messy bun. She plodded down the stairs and into the kitchen, opening the cabinet where the cereal was stored. Some people might think it odd to eat cereal in the early afternoon, but with Aubrey's different schedule at the hospital, this was something she did more often than not.

Once she'd poured milk over the cereal in a large bowl, she brought it over to the island and grabbed a spoon from the drawer in the process. She'd taken a few bites before she heard the front door opening.

"Oh good. You're up!" Aubrey's mom grinned at her, wiping at the moisture on her forehead. She was dressed in jeans and a button-up shirt, her uniform for working outdoors on the ranch.

"Yeah, I just woke up. What's everyone up to?" With another bite of sugared cereal in her mouth, Aubrey looked at her mom, waiting for an answer.

With a chuckle, her mom said, "Evan thought it would be a good idea to muck out the horse stalls today. The guys are never going to let him plan a reunion again, I'm afraid."

Pointing her spoon at her mom, Aubrey said, "That might have been Evan's whole point. Unless he can compare a dirty horse stall to business somehow."

"I wouldn't put it past him," her mom said, grinning. Evan had always been good at negotiating, but even this would be a stretch. "When you're done, come out and see what they're up to. It's almost funny to watch them all work."

Aubrey grinned, picturing the arrogant Italian guy from the night before. She could use something to ease her bruised ego.

Her mom pulled out a tray and loaded it with several bottles of water. "When you're done with that, why don't you take these out to the guys? It's a bit warmer today, and with all the work they're putting in, I'm sure they could use it."

"You don't want to do that?" Aubrey asked, hiding a smile as she stuffed another spoonful into her mouth. She knew her mother's motives, and she wasn't sure she wanted to be a part of it, not wanting to get involved with any of the billionaires. There were a lot of people who clamored for their attention as it was, hoping to get some part of their money. Aubrey was less interested in it than anyone, knowing that with all that wealth had come a lot of negative effects to her brothers' lives.

Her mother frowned. "No, I've got to get dinner going right now. It takes longer to feed this many people."

Aubrey finished the milk in her bowl. After rinsing it out and putting it in the dishwasher, she debated whether or not to run up and change her clothes. But the ultra-casual look might be a better deterrent than anything.

She moved to the door with the tray of waters. At the front door, she slipped on the Crocs she used as part of her nursing uniform. Taking slow steps, she walked out the door and down the porch steps, heading in the direction of the stables.

The guys were all standing around watching something, several of them with their hand on their shovel. She saw Aiden and went to stand next to him, peering around the others to see two guys, each in their own stall.

Evan was holding up his phone, glancing between the guys and the screen every few seconds.

"What's going on?" she asked Aiden.

He shook his head and pointed. "Max and Gabe decided to have a friendly competition to see who could clean out the stall the fastest."

Aubrey watched as the guys moved their shovels, little

piles of brown dirt flying everywhere. "It looks like they're making more of a mess than actually cleaning it up."

Aiden gave her a nod and a knowing look. He reached over and took a water from the tray, giving her a grateful smile as he unscrewed the lid. She held the tray out in front of some of the others, and they all did the same thing.

The group watched in silence, a comment escaping every once in a while. Aubrey noticed the muscles on Gabe's back moving with the effort of shoveling. He was built well, his upper body visible through the thin long-sleeved t-shirt he wore. His dark hair and dark eyes were something that had always been her kryptonite, but after meeting the guy the night before, she knew she needed to keep her distance from this one. Competitive or not, attractive or not, she just needed to stay focused on…well, she didn't have much else to think about at the moment.

After another minute of watching, Gabe stood up with his hands in the air, looking as if he'd just won a major award.

"Finito." He stepped out of the stall and rested his chin on the top of the shovel handle. He glanced around and locked eyes with Aubrey, his smile slipping a bit but the intensity of his gaze making her squirm. Why she even came out here in the first place, she didn't know, but she just needed to relax and then head back to California, back to real life where she was Aubrey the single nurse, and just accept that as her reality.

Evan walked through the stall, inspecting Gabe's work. "You didn't get it spotless, but it's a lot better than it looked at the beginning."

Max walked out of his stall, wiping at his brow despite the cool January air. "Gabe's a cheat. Half of his stuff ended up on my side several times."

"Please, all my dirt and excrement is in the wheelbarrow. I wouldn't have tried to sabotage the game."

Aubrey was surprised. Was he really being sincere? From the night before, she could imagine he was one of those people who did everything they could to win, even if it meant hurting someone else. Aubrey liked to win at cards, but as hard as it was for her to swallow defeat, she knew the limits of when to pursue further and when to hang back.

Gabe leaned his shovel against the side of the stall and walked in Aubrey's direction. He didn't take his eyes from hers as he took a water bottle from the tray. After taking a long swig, he swallowed and said, "Thank you, Aubrey. It was so kind of you to bring the champion some water."

Aubrey rolled her eyes, turning toward Max and handing him a water. She was not about to give this guy the impression that he had any kind of effect on her.

"What's on the agenda now, Evan?" Gabe asked before taking a long draw of his water.

"I thought I'd leave it up to you guys for this afternoon. We have horses you can take on a trail ride up into the mountains behind the ranch, or we have an archery range just on the other side of the stalls." Evan looked around at the group. "You could swim in the pond, but you'd have to break the ice to do that." His words caused a chuckle to pass through the crowd, and they slowly dispersed in different directions, some back to the house and others to the archery range.

Gabe's voice startled Aubrey as she thought he'd moved off with the rest of the group. "What are you up to this afternoon?" He drank some of his water, and Aubrey got the impression he was waiting to decide what he would do depending on her answer.

Folding her arms across her chest, Aubrey tilted her head to the side, her eyebrows scrunched together as she studied him. "I'm not really sure I'll do anything yet. This isn't my reunion." She gave a quick smile and walked past him to the house. She'd come looking for a sanctuary from her real life, and she knew the perfect place to find some peace without all the guys around.

CHAPTER 7

Gabe watched as Aubrey walked away, his jaw slack from her comment. She must have known he was curious about what she'd do with her time, but he felt a strange pull to her, and his senses seemed to heighten when she was around.

"Let's go for a ride, shall we?" Max slapped him on the back and flashed him a smile.

"What kind of ride?"

"On horseback. It will be good to get out of the lodge for longer than an hour." Max moved in the direction of the large log building where they'd been staying.

Gabe glanced back over his shoulder, no Aubrey in sight. Shrugging, he followed Max, knowing that a ride might be good for him. It was something he hadn't had a chance to do for years, and he needed to take advantage of all the little things while he had the chance.

Twenty minutes later, he and Max mounted their horses, along with Aiden and Sam, prepared with adequate clothing for the forty-degree weather. Still, Gabe shivered in his coat, two thermal shirts, and a wool scarf. He wasn't used to this kind of cold in Venice, and he was just glad he'd brought this much.

The rain and snow from the day before made the ground soft, and the first few steps of the horse on the path caused his insides to turn. He clung to the reins and hoped he and the horse wouldn't slip down into the mud. He wasn't the most proficient rider, as he'd only done it a few times as a child.

"Are we all ready to go?" Aiden asked.

The other three nodded. Gabe hung back a bit, letting a few of the other guys go before him. He didn't need to be teased about his deficient horse-riding skills.

The horses climbed up a steep hill, and Gabe focused on his horse and staying upright in the saddle. He was used to navigating a boat around some of the narrowest stretches of water in Venice and could do it in his sleep. Riding a horse took more brainpower than he'd thought.

After nearly thirty minutes, they made it to a clearing, and Aiden navigated his horse to allow the others to edge forward, giving the guys' horses a break for a few minutes on the flat terrain.

"Okay, so this is what we call The Grove. It's a great spot to hang out, especially in the summertime because the air is a bit cooler up here and there is plenty of space for a party. We arrange parties up here for people staying at the lodge quite a bit during the summer months." He pulled on his reins, and the horse took a few steps back, giving everyone a view.

It wasn't green right then, but Gabe could imagine what it would be like covered in leaves. From the angle of some of the branches, it would create a canopy, shielding the travelers from the harshness of the sun.

"How long has your family lived on the ranch?" Sam asked, pulling down the scarf around his face. The poor guy was used to the warm weather of South America, and even this barely-above-freezing temperature was making it hard for him. Gabe was only faring a little better at the moment, blowing hot air into his hands and rubbing them together. He should have asked to borrow some gloves.

"Our grandfather started it when he and my grandmother first married. It was more of a working ranch than anything at that point. When our father grew up, he helped build some of the buildings, like the lodge and the bunkhouse." The pride in Aiden's voice was evident. "Let's keep moving along. If we want to make it to the falls and back before dark, we need to pick up the pace."

As they worked their way up a steeper portion of the hill, Gabe took in the beauty of the mountainside. Even with everything asleep for winter, the scenery was varied with pine trees and white aspens. The landscape seemed so peaceful, and it eased another knot of tension from his shoulders.

Another twenty minutes, and they had made it to a spot that opened up to a large waterfall. Aiden instructed them all to dismount and tie up their horses. Gabe slid off, grateful to be on solid ground, but was caught off guard when he saw an extra horse tied up to the fence keeping the horses out of the pool at the bottom of the falls.

They moved behind Aiden, who followed a trail on foot in between several trees, wrapping around to a larger lookout of the waterfall. A familiar figure stood leaning up against the railing with her hair in the same high ponytail but dressed differently than sweats. Her jeans were cut just right to her curves, and the thick coat she wore looked like it would do the trick of keeping out the cold.

The other three men lined up on her left side, talking about the falls while Aiden gave them several answers on the facts of the waterfall and the surrounding area. Gabe slid in next to Aubrey's right side, and she glanced over at him, her facial expression appearing as though she'd just eaten something sour.

"You rode a horse up here?" she asked, her body language telling him it was hard for her to believe.

"Yes, and I did a pretty good job of it if I do say so myself." Gabe let the corners of his mouth turn up, his attention focused on her reaction.

Aubrey rolled her eyes and said, "Of course. Why did I expect any other answer?" She turned her attention back to the waterfall. The reflection of the water in her eyes mesmerized Gabe, and it was several seconds before he realized he should really focus on something else so he didn't creep her out.

"To tell you the truth, I'm surprised I made it up here. I haven't ridden a horse in years, and it was a bit harder than trying to ride a bike again." He didn't look at her, but he could see a small smile on her face in his peripheral vision.

"I can understand that," she said, her voice warmer than he'd heard it in the past two days. "Riding a bike all depends on you, but horses are alive and have a mind of their own. I was bucked off a few times while growing up, and as much as I didn't want to at the time, getting back on the horse was so important for my mental state when it came to horses. We have really good horses, though, so you should be safe." She smiled at him and turned her gaze back to the water.

Gabe let the silence settle for a few moments and then said, "There's something about water, isn't there?"

"What?"

"Something calming about it. Where I live, we're surrounded by water, and it's amazing what a little boat ride will do to help me unwind after a long day."

She nodded. "This has always been one of my favorite spots to think. It just seems that the water helps all the thoughts fall into place."

"Am I interrupting your silence, then?" Gabe asked, sliding a few feet away. He did his best to keep the smile off his face, turning to her with eyebrows raised and what he considered his innocent face.

Aubrey giggled, the light sound sinking into his chest and making his heart pound against his ribcage. He hadn't felt the gurgling of excitement in his stomach like this in over a decade, and his emotions mixed with the thoughts of his high school sweetheart and the girl standing in front of him.

"No, you're good. I think I figured out most of it before you guys got here."

Gabe waited a few seconds and slid back over, bumping into her shoulder and causing her to giggle again. What seemed to be the hard outer shell he'd seen since she appeared in her parents' home the night before was nearly crumbling before his eyes as she continued to smile, the action causing her eyes to twinkle.

"We should probably head back," Aiden said, breaking the moment of magic between Gabe and Aubrey. "I'm sure Mom's got another feast prepared for us, and we wouldn't want the others to eat it all."

Gabe nodded. If there was one thing he knew from the past twenty-four hours at the Pearson home, it was that Terri Pearson knew how to cook. And bake. His mouth watered just thinking about the sugar cookies she'd made for them. He just hoped the other guys hadn't eaten them all by the time they got back.

The group was silent as they walked down the short path to their horses. It took two tries for Gabe to mount his horse, and he glanced around, grateful no one else had noticed, most of all Aubrey.

They made their way back, the only sound the consistent plodding of the horses' hooves. Gabe looked around, his focus on the landscape around him.

"Look out!" came a voice from up ahead.

Gabe whipped his head toward the front, his body tensing as he saw one of the horses in front rear back. Holding on to the reins, Gabe pulled his horse to the side, trying to move enough to be out of the way of the other horses in front. The prick of the branches made it through his coat as he watched the horse buck the rider off.

Max.

His body landed on a large rock, the crack of his head against it causing Gabe's stomach to lurch. He slid down, moving around the horses to get to his friend. By the time he was there, Aubrey was already at Max's side, checking his pulse and pupils. The other guys were huddled around, and Gabe watched as she worked her way through the check, her calm floating in the air.

Max's eyes opened, and he looked at them all, dazed.

"How are you feeling?" Aubrey asked him.

Blinking a few times, Max said, "Just a headache." He pushed to a sitting position, keeping his hand on the side of his head.

"Can you feel your feet, toes, fingers?" Aubrey asked.

Max nodded. "It's all a bit sore, but I can feel it."

Aubrey blew out a deep breath and smiled. As Gabe watched her, some of the panic he'd felt melted away. "Do you know what made the horse rear back?"

With a shake of the head, Max said, "I'm not exactly sure, but I saw something moving in the bushes out of the corner of my eye. Whatever it was spooked the horse."

"Okay, do you think you can mount your horse again? We need to get you down to the lodge to keep an eye on you for right now."

Gabe helped support Max as he pushed off the ground. It took a moment for his friend to get his foot into the stirrup and over the middle of the horse, but he finally settled in.

Aubrey turned to Aiden and gave some instructions that Gabe couldn't hear before mounting her horse and turning it around.

"How are you, buddy?" Gabe asked after he'd mounted his horse and moved up beside him.

Max rolled his eyes. "I'll be fine. I'm ready for a nap, though." He chuckled, the sound more like a sputter.

"We'll need to keep him awake for the trip down," Aubrey said, looking Gabe in the eyes.

"Okay, I can do that." He nudged his horse along the path. "What embarrassing stories should we relate for Aubrey?" He grinned, watching her reaction.

To his surprise, she laughed and shook her head. "I guess that's one way to do it." She moved her head so she could see Max's eyes one more time before the path narrowed, only allowing one horse at a time. "Just make sure everything is good in back, will you, boys?"

Gabe looked back at Aiden and Sam, their expressions solemn.

The way she'd handled the whole situation made him grateful she'd been there. He had only a basic knowledge of first aid, and as he thought about each of the guys, none of them really knew much about the medical field. They were lucky she'd been on the trail with them.

His eyes locked with Aubrey's for several seconds, pulling feelings to the surface that Gabe hadn't felt in a long time. Not since the girl he'd loved since kinder had passed away during his freshman year of college. The thought of Nicoletta reminded him of why he'd kept his heart so well-guarded for the past twelve years. As much as he'd felt for Aubrey in their brief interactions, it was just something that would pass, and then he could go back to the way things were before.

He wasn't lucky enough to find love twice.

CHAPTER 8

*A*ubrey checked on Max throughout the night and all day Saturday. He said he only had a slight headache and wasn't exhibiting any other signs of a concussion, but she didn't know if that would change with a bit more time. With as hard as his head cracked against the rock, he'd be lucky to make it without at least a concussion.

It was Sunday afternoon, and she was already packing up, knowing she'd have to drive back to California in a few hours to give her enough time to sleep for her shift the next night.

As she pulled a few of her clothes from the closet, her eyes caught on the shelf above the closet rod. She reached up and pulled down an old three-ring binder. It had been a while since she'd seen it, and as she opened it, some of the pages stuck together from the magazine clippings inside.

It was the book she and Sadie had worked for years to put together, starting when they were in second grade. Aubrey would smuggle up some of her mother's old magazines, and the two of them would comb through them, cutting out the things they wanted to achieve or see or do in their lives. The reminder of years of poring over these pages, dreaming of how they would get there, caused tears to form in her eyes.

As Aubrey scanned each of the pictures, she realized that some of her dreams had already been fulfilled. She'd graduated from college and become a nurse, just like she'd wanted for so long. And Sadie had been able to travel to far-off places, planning weddings for people. She'd even gotten married, which was funny as she'd drawn a large blue X through a picture of a bride on one of her pages.

Aubrey gasped as she turned the next page, seeing a family smiling back at her. She was only thirty. She'd be okay, and she loved her life. But the loneliness was getting worse by the day. Maybe she just needed to find a new friend, one she could go to movies with and catch up over dinner.

The next page was filled with cathedrals and lots of European buildings. While Sadie had wanted to travel to some of the bigger cities, it had always been Aubrey's dream to go to Europe to see all the beautiful architecture and experience the cultures there. She'd always wanted to but had never gone.

An idea settled in her chest and began to grow, her mind spinning with the ideas. What if she took time off and went now? Sure, it wasn't as fun as going with friends, but she needed a break from her life, needed a break from the monotony, and traveling through Europe would be the perfect way to do that.

She already had a passport from her various excursions to Mexico with Sadie, so that was one less thing she needed to get. All she'd need to do was research flights, hotels, and transportation. It might seem daunting for some, but the idea excited her more than anything else had done in months.

Checking the time, she realized she needed to get going.

She slid the binder back on the shelf and grabbed her bag, taking quick steps down the stairs.

The door from the half-bath opened, and Gabe walked out, adjusting his watch on his arm. Not wanting him to see her excitement, she did her best to avoid his gaze.

"Heading out?" he asked.

Aubrey looked up, noting a smile playing on his lips. A tingle ran up her back and through her arms, causing her to shudder. She shoved it back, reminding herself what the perfect guy would look like for her. Someone who would be a good husband and father, one who would be her best friend and not always put himself above her. From everything she'd learned about Gabe in the past four days, he cared about his friends. But he did it all with an air about him, and Aubrey couldn't imagine dealing with that forever.

But the time they'd spent by the waterfall had been enjoyable, and some of his comments had been really funny. Maybe there was something underneath the tough shell he presented to the world. Too bad she didn't have the time to crack it. As much as he drove her crazy, she was attracted to him, more than she wanted to admit.

"Yes, I need to get back to the hospital. How about you? Are you heading home soon?" She set her bag on the floor and leaned against the counter, folding her arms as if to tell her beating heart that it was off-limits to this dark-haired, olive-skinned Italian model.

Gabe smiled and nodded his head. "Yes, it's a quick trip, but it's worth it to see all the guys. Are you trying to get rid of me already?" His eyebrows wriggled.

Aubrey rolled her eyes. "No, I was just curious. I wasn't sure if you're just a playboy back in Rome or if you actually work." Aubrey tilted her chin up half an inch and stared into his eyes, signaling the challenge.

He took a few steps closer, stopping about a foot away

from her. The movement caused the smell of sandalwood to wrap itself around her, and she had to work to not visibly inhale. He leaned his hand on the counter to Aubrey's side and said, "Actually, I live in Venice, not Rome. They're a few hours apart. And as far as being a playboy, I'm the furthest thing from that. Unless you count the number of dates my mother has set me up on." Sadness shadowed his eyes as he leaned back, and Aubrey wondered what that meant.

"Well, you're braver than I am, then. My mother has offered several times, but I don't know if I don't trust her judgment or if I'm just too proud to let her." She laughed, her words sinking into her own mind. The realization was like a cold bucket of water on her head, but what else had she been too stubborn to accept in her life?

Gabe gave her a half-smile, moving to lean up against the counter next to her. His shoulder touched hers, and she felt waves of excitement pour through her. "If you met my mother, you'd know I didn't really have a choice. But it's probably good. It gets me away from my work."

"So you've never been in a relationship before?" Aubrey clapped her hand over her mouth, surprised that she'd even asked such a blunt question.

His eyes got a faraway look, and he gave a curt nod. "Once, a long time ago."

Aubrey's mom came into the room and pulled out a few pans. She turned around and jumped a bit when she saw the two of them standing there. After a few seconds, a smile spread across her face as she looked between the two of them.

"I didn't realize you were in here. I'm just getting dinner started. Aubrey, are you staying?" Her mother's eyes were wide open, trying to ask more than that with her body language.

Taking a step away from the counter, Aubrey missed the

sensation that Gabe's shoulder brought her and shook her head. "No, I'd better get going before it gets dark. I think I'll just take a few of the snacks in the pantry."

"Would you like help bringing your luggage downstairs?" Gabe asked, his expression more genuine than she'd seen so far.

With a slight smile, Aubrey picked up her bag. "This is all I have. But thank you." She turned and moved to the pantry to find some food, focusing on the task of getting on the road and not the sincerity of his light chocolate-brown eyes.

CHAPTER 9

"Back to work," Gabe said as he exited his private jet on the following Saturday. The group had stayed another five days at Silver Ridge Ranch before they'd headed back home. The flight time and time change had robbed him of another day, and Gabe knew it was going to take a few days before the jet lag would pass.

He secured the hangar and jumped in his sports car to begin the few kilometer ride to Marghera. It was early evening, and as much as he knew his mother would want him to come home for family dinner, he was just ready for bed.

The traffic was fairly light, and he made it to his boat in under a quarter of an hour. The docks were busier than the streets, several people coming in after a day out on the water. Just one more trip, and he'd be able to relax in his apartment, giving himself enough time to rest before work on Monday. With the amount of exhaustion in his limbs, he knew he was going to need every bit to recover from the past week.

As he navigated the water, he reflected on his trip to Silver Ridge Ranch. As much as he'd wanted to have the retreat on a beach somewhere, he was surprisingly pleased with how well it had gone. It had been the perfect amount of physical labor and relaxing fun, not to mention he'd officially met Aubrey Pearson.

He pictured her dark hair and her piercing blue eyes. The way her lips puckered when he'd said something to annoy her. And the way he'd felt when their shoulders touched in the kitchen. It seemed like such a small thing to focus on, but when he hadn't felt like that in years, the sensation seemed heightened.

If only they lived closer to each other. But taking an American girl from her tight-knit family would be as hard as pulling him from his own. What he needed to focus on now was hiring people to take over, giving him the opportunity to make bigger personal decisions.

After arriving at the island of Venice, he tied up his boat and pulled his bags out, walking the short distance to his apartment. Peace and quiet was all he wanted after a week of men chatting about everything under the sun.

As he moved in front of his door, his hand stretched out to unlock the door, he heard voices on the other side. Who would be in his home? The aroma of pasta and sauce, with garlic and basil floated toward him, and all hopes of being alone for the night were gone.

Walking inside, he set his bag on the couch next to where his father had fallen asleep with a book on his chest. Voices came from the kitchen, and Gabe moved in that direction.

"Mom, what are you all doing here?" He leaned against the doorframe and folded his arms across his chest.

The small woman in front of the stove turned and grinned at him. Her arm was stirring something in a big pot, and the rest of the stovetop was covered in other pots and pans, the kitchen looking like it had exploded based on the amount of food on the counters.

"We thought we'd have dinner here, just in case you were hungry when you landed. How was your trip?" She cut up several vegetables, her hands cutting through each at a speed that was still amazing for Gabe after thirty years.

"It was good. I was hoping to just head to bed, though."

His mother tsked and said, "Not without a proper meal." She paused a moment, looking him up and down. "Please tell me you wore a coat or a scarf when you drove the boat here."

Gabe looked down, seeing his long-sleeved shirt. Normally he would have remembered to dress warmer for the cool air, but he'd been so focused on getting home that he'd forgotten. He pictured Aubrey teasing him about the amount of layers he'd worn and chuckled.

"I just got out of the car and into the boat." He rubbed a hand over his face, trying to prepare himself for the lecture that was to come. "It was only a few minutes and felt good, considering the long flight I'd just taken."

"Gabriele Giovanni Alessandro, you know better than to traipse around in the winter with only a t-shirt. You'll catch a cold, and then I'll find out you've been admitted to the hospital for pneumonia." The deep line in her forehead showed just how much she worried about Gabe and Sophia. As much as he wanted to laugh about the jump from cold to serious illness, he knew there was no changing her thought process.

Footsteps came bounding into the kitchen, and he turned to find his younger sister, Sophia, smiling up at him. They kissed each other on the cheeks, and she gave him a hug. At only five foot seven, Sophia was small but fierce, her spunk now reminding him of Aubrey.

"It's about time you got back. Mom's been worried about you flying across the ocean again." She made an exaggerated fainting motion.

Gabe chuckled, knowing it might not be far from the

truth. "That's why you're supposed to distract her with your antics. No school right now, huh?"

She raised one eyebrow, looking at him as though he'd lost his mind. "You do remember it's the weekend, right?" Standing on tiptoe, she felt his forehead with the back of her hand. A mischievous smile crossed her face, and she turned to their mother. "Mom, I think Gabe has a fever."

Their mother's eyes went wide, and she wiped her hands off on a dishtowel before coming over and placed her hand on his forehead. "You do feel a bit warm. Maybe you should sit down."

"Mom," Gabe said, trying to keep the exasperation out of his voice. "I'm fine. Sophia is just teasing. I'll make sure to rest after dinner once you all go home."

It took a few seconds of looking innocent, but his mother finally agreed, turning back to the kitchen. "Come help set the table, you two. The food is about ready."

Fifteen minutes later, the four of them were sitting at the small dining table that had been handed down from his grandparents. It was too small to use for entertaining at his parents' home, but it was just the right size for his apartment, and Gabe knew how much it meant to his mother to keep it around.

After the antipasti, his mother served what they called primo, usually pasta. It was as delicious as ever, and he was grateful he'd grown up with a great cook. He'd learned bits and pieces from her over the years, enough to survive for dinner throughout the week. Terri Pearson had made some delicious meals as well, some of them he'd never tried before.

"How was the reunion, Gabe?" his father asked as he cut a piece of chicken during the second portion of dinner.

"Really good. It was what I needed. The chance to relax for a bit and talk shop with my friends." Gabe chewed on a piece of chicken and realized his words as he glanced at his father's downturned face. "Dad, it's fine. Once a year is good for me to get out like that. But I know how important this company is to our family and to the community."

His father wiped the corners of his mouth with a napkin, the tension in his jaw showing how much he was struggling with whatever he needed to say. "I'm just sorry I can't be of more help to you, son. I know how hard you work, how many hours you put in. I didn't build this company to make it so you couldn't have a social life and never get away."

"I know, Dad." It was the same conversation they'd had over and over, but Gabe hadn't yet found a way to get his father to relax and not worry about the company so much. He looked him in the eyes, hoping to convince him this time. "But I think it's time we find some people to hire that we trust. It might take a little longer than just one interview to vet them, but I think that will help give us all a little breathing room."

Sophia raised her hand. "I'd like to be one of those people."

The other three turned to look at her. Gabe tried to read her face, wondering if this was some strange joke, because joking was her thing.

"What about university? You can't just give up after two years," their mother chided.

"There are plenty of online courses I can take to finish my degree, and I'll get on-the-job training in the process." Sophia smiled hesitantly at Gabe as if pleading with him to side with her.

Gabe finished his chicken, his mind spinning with the reasons why his sister would want to leave her university in Bologna to stay home in Venice. But he'd thought about how she'd make a great employee for the company when he was in America. He shouldn't hesitate now that she was willing this early.

Finally, he said, "If that's what you want to do, I'd be grateful for the help." With the eight years of age difference between the two of them, he didn't always understand her, but she looked like this was something she needed right now.

His mother let out an exasperated sigh, and his father focused on his plate once more. Soon enough, dinner was over, and Gabe and Sophia were in the kitchen doing the dishes.

"Why do you really want to work for Cristallo, Sof?" Gabe asked as he scrubbed one of the large pots his mother had used.

"I want to. I know how hard you work, and Mom said she's worried you're going to suffer a heart attack just like Dad in the next few years because you work too much. You don't get a break hardly ever. And to be honest, I'm bored." She sighed. "I can juggle online classes and a full-time job, and it will help that it's actually a valuable job, helping people around me instead of just in retail like most of the girls I know do."

Gabe paused a minute before handing the plate to her. She ran it under the rinse water and wiped it off. He'd thought about putting in a dishwasher when he moved in, but there weren't that many dishes to do for one person, and he liked these little moments of bonding over the dishes.

"Okay, if that's all it is."

"Promise. Now, anything interesting happen in Utah? Did you meet any girls?" Sophia's eyebrows fluttered as a wide smile crossed her face.

"N—well, one girl. It was Evan's triplet sister, Aubrey. I don't think she likes me too much though. I was kind of obnoxious." He smirked.

Sophia stopped wiping the large pot. "Please tell me you didn't play card games with her."

Gabe nodded guiltily. "She's pretty competitive, but I beat

her a few times. It was kind of fun to watch." He felt a sharp jab to his shoulder and saw Sophia pulling her fist away.

"Really? What are you? Ten years old? You need to find a girl to settle down with, but you never will if you're being immature and annoying." Her tone softened when she spoke again. "Is she pretty?"

"Yes, and I wasn't all bad. We had a few good moments here and there." He recalled her laugh while next to the waterfall, and a pang of sadness hit him square in the chest. Sophia had stopped drying to stare at him, and he continued. "She's a nurse in California. But we live on opposite sides of the world, so there's no way that's going to work out."

"Why not? If you like each other, long-distance won't matter."

Gabe pulled his hand out of the soapy water and touched her nose, leaving a puff of white behind. "Says the girl who's moving back home to see her ex-boyfriend."

Sophia's mouth went slack for a few seconds before she said, "That's not the reason. But it would be a nice benefit." She moved to put one of the pans away in the cupboard and turned back to him. "What have you got to lose? If you're interested in her, get her number from Evan. The worst that could happen is she turns you down. But then you don't have to wonder what could have happened."

Her words ran circles around Gabe's mind, and he just nodded, trying to decide if he was up for the effort. The next day was going to be packed with all the things he needed to catch up on, and he told himself if he remembered after that, he'd give it a try.

CHAPTER 10

Aubrey got off the train when it arrived in Venice at seven in the morning on a Thursday. She'd finished out the three shifts she was scheduled for the week after leaving Silver Ridge Ranch and had asked for time off, leaving on a plane the next day for Paris.

The plane ride was long, but the jet lag was what took its toll those first few days. She'd been in Europe now for six days of her three-week trip and had enjoyed every moment. In each of the major cities, she'd found a tour group, learning about the history of each place they walked past. She'd arrived from Florence, probably her favorite place so far, but as she looked around at the beautiful clear water of Venice, it took her breath away, and she knew her partiality was about to change.

She picked up a map of the city at the train station, rubbing her neck as she studied it. At the beginning of her trip, she'd decided taking night trains would be worthwhile as she wouldn't have to pay for a hostel every night and would be able to enjoy the scenery without taking the whole day for travel. After last night's ride, she made the decision that she was going to get a hostel bed for the night just so her body could rest without being constantly woken up by other passengers or the train employees checking passports.

Pulling out her list of places she'd researched to visit, she looked for each on the map, trying to decide which one to see first and where everything was in connection to the rest. San Marco Piazza was her first destination, and she began walking through the streets, admiring the beauty of the buildings she passed, and was surprised by how many bridges went over water as she made her way through the city.

She bought a pastry from one of the only places open that early, just then realizing how few people she'd seen since she'd arrived. It only took a few more minutes before she reached the square, but the beauty of the place amazed her.

It was a rectangular courtyard surrounded by several-story buildings, and at the one end stood a large church, San Marco Basilica from what the map said. The architecture and colors of the building made her wish she'd been some sort of art history major so she could accurately explain each and every detail.

She considered sitting out on a bench in the piazza, when the bright blue of the ocean to her right caught her eye. Strolling out, she saw a row of gondolas lined up, a few men milling about them. It looked like the prime location for a romance movie, and she grinned at the thought.

Movement to her left caught her eye, and she glanced over at a man running along the boardwalk. She gave a slight smile before turning back to her pastry and the ocean, mesmerized by the beauty of the still-rising sun.

"Aubrey?" a deep familiar voice asked a few feet away. She turned to see that the runner was Gabe dressed in sweats and a sweatshirt with a beanie, sweat pouring down the sides of his face. The weather was a little brisk, but running with that much clothing on would make her uncomfortable, especially once she'd warmed up.

"Gabe. I-I didn't expect to see you here." The shock seemed to affect her tongue, and she couldn't figure out what else to say. It didn't take long, though, and the words tumbled out of her mouth. "Why do you look like the Abominable Snowman?"

"I do live here. And it's cold out. You're only wearing a coat." He unwrapped his scarf and wrapped it around her, the smell of his cologne surprising her. "What are you doing in Venice?" He moved back and forth from leg to leg, his chest heaving as he worked to breathe.

Aubrey smiled, realizing that she would be more of a surprise. "I needed a break from life in California. I've always wanted to tour Europe, so here I am." She stretched her hands out to her sides and smiled.

"Is Venice your first stop?" She watched as his eyes studied her face, something indiscernible in his expression.

She shook her head. "No, I flew to Paris and Rome and then took trains to Florence and now here." The way he was looking at her made her blush and look away, surprised at the attention and manners he had.

"How long are you here? I'd love to show you around." He smiled, his white teeth contrasting against his sun-kissed skin, making her legs feel like jelly.

"Well, I don't have anything set for the next couple days yet, and then I have about two weeks left to explore the rest of Europe. I was planning to find a hostel for the night to get some more rest."

He reached out and touched her hand, the sensation sending tingles all the way to her elbow. "You can stay with my family. My sister would love to meet you."

Raising an eyebrow, Aubrey chuckled a bit. "Why would she even know who I am?"

Gabe's eyes widened for a split second before his usual calm demeanor settled over his features. "She likes to keep tabs on all the guys from the International Billionaire Club. When I told her Evan and Aiden were triplets, she's been fascinated ever since."

That sounded almost credible.

"Well, if you don't think it would be too much trouble, I'd enjoy staying with your family." Her statement caused her to wonder if Gabe still lived with his parents. A thirty-year-old still living at home seemed a little odd for a billionaire, but then again, the customs were different here.

Gabe grinned again. He looked down at her suitcase and back up to her face. "Is that all you brought?"

Aubrey laughed. "Yes, I figured I'd have to have it with me for the most part, and it's nice that it's a little bigger than a carry-on so I don't have trouble loading it into and out of cars, trains, etc."

"That's impressive. Sophia would probably have five bags if she were to go to the States for any length of time. Let me take that for you." He moved his hand next to hers on the suitcase, his hand feeling like a warm fire next to her chilled hands.

What was her deal? She couldn't like someone that lived thousands of miles away from where she lived. Her last boyfriend, Lance, had moved to Chicago, and they'd only made it a month before they called their relationship off. Then again, he had cheated on her. But she was having the time of her life. There was nothing wrong with being attracted to someone, even if he was arrogant, for a day or two, or at least until she went home and got back to life.

Maybe that was her problem. She tended to judge people from the first few meetings and that could be why she hadn't fulfilled her dreams of marriage and a family yet. Allowing herself some time to have fun here might help her in the long run.

He waved for her to follow and headed into the piazza before turning back through one of the streets and weaving for some time. "If you don't mind, I just need a quick shower, and then we'll head over to Marghera. That's where my company, Cristallo, is and where my family lives."

Aubrey remembered that today was still a weekday. "Don't you have to work today? I don't want to pull you away if you have stuff to do."

They were walking side by side at that point, and he turned his head, giving her a half-smile. "I'd much rather play tour guide with you today. I've been working long days since I got back from the ranch, and I could use a good distraction." He winked at her and faced forward again, sending chills running throughout Aubrey's body. She'd been winked at by plenty of men over the years, but for the first time, she didn't want to throw up because of it.

A few minutes later, he stopped before a large building and opened the door with a key. He held it open and motioned for her to pass first, surprising her even more. He was a lot more gentlemanly than she'd expected, just like her brothers. They walked up five flights of stairs, and Aubrey was grateful when there were no more.

"With that kind of a hike, it's a wonder you even have to go jogging. Are you sweating through all those layers?" Aubrey asked, trying to mask her mischievous smile.

"Well, my American friend, Italians are a bit worried about catching a cold, so we tend to make sure we're always covered, especially when exercising in the cold." He raised an eyebrow as if asking whether that answer was sufficient or not.

Shaking her head, Aubrey said, "Well, you might be a little crazy, but that's a valid concern." She pointed to the two doors down the hallway and asked, "Only two apartments are on this floor?"

"Used to be. I bought both and knocked out one of the walls between them to make it bigger." Gabe's response seemed sheepish, as though he were a little embarrassed by the answer. They walked into his flat, and Aubrey was amazed. There were windows all around, showing off the landscape of buildings across Venice.

"This is amazing." She walked up to the window and looked down, seeing the tops of several buildings.

"Thanks. I've always loved Venice. So a couple years after graduating from Hawthorne, I decided it was time to move out and find my own place. I renovated this, and it's been pretty perfect." He stuffed his hands into his sweatshirt pouch and grinned at her.

"You have some good taste." Aubrey walked along, admiring the beautiful art on the walls.

"Let me take a quick shower, and then we can get going."

Gabe ducked out of the room, and Aubrey giggled softly. It seemed as though her being there was throwing off everything for him, which she didn't mind. This relaxed side of Gabe was much better than the arrogant side she'd seen in Aspen Hollow, even though they'd had a few good moments together.

There were several pictures on the mantel of people who looked a lot like Gabe's family, smiling or laughing in every picture. They must be close. The thought made her miss her own family. But they were all spread out over the US now and didn't get much time together.

Within a few minutes, Gabe reappeared in slacks and a polo, pulling on a thick wool coat. Seeing him freshly shaven and clean, Aubrey had to look at the floor so he wouldn't see the heat rushing to her ears.

"Are you ready to go?" he asked.

"Yep." She let the p pop and stood with a smile, grateful she had composed herself.

He looked her up and down before asking, "Do you need a scarf or anything?"

"No, I should be good. The weather isn't too bad compared to the snow I've been through."

"Are you sure?"

Aubrey grinned at him, tilting her head a bit to show him she was sure. "I'll be fine. Lead out, Tour Guide Gabe."

He flashed that half-smile again. "That has a nice ring to it."

Aubrey nodded, agreeing with him. Of all the chance encounters in the world, she was still amazed that she'd been able to meet up with probably the only acquaintance she had in Venice. And it wouldn't be too bad if she got to hang out with him all day looking like that either.

CHAPTER 11

As Gabe steered the boat into his slip at the docks along Marghera a few minutes later, he still couldn't believe Aubrey was here. He'd thought about her a lot over the past two weeks, but since he'd returned home, every time he'd thought about calling Evan, it had been the middle of the night Mountain Time, and he'd get too busy and forget later.

He turned off the engine to the boat and then stepped onto the dock. Reaching for her hand, he helped pull Aubrey out of the boat. The electricity flowing through their hands seemed even stronger than when he'd touched her hand while taking her suitcase. Wheeling the bag behind him now, he bent his arm and offered it to her, liking the feel of her so close to him as she slid her arm through his. They made their way to the end of the dock near some large factory buildings and walked up onto the walkway.

"So, is this still considered Venice?" Aubrey asked, motioning around them.

"Venice province. But the capitol of the province is Venice, which is where we were."

Aubrey looked at him, and he could see the wheels turning in her head. "So provinces are kind of like our states?"

"Yep. Each one has a capitol." He pulled open the door to his factory and let her go ahead of him, a light vanilla scent hitting him as she walked by.

"Where are we?" she asked.

Gabe blinked a few times to allow his eyes to adjust to the darkness inside. There were still several lights on overhead, but their brightness wasn't as intense as the sun.

Gabe grinned. "This is my family's factory. We produce just about everything here and send it all over the world."

He reached for her hand, and they walked through another door and up two flights of stairs. Leading her into his office, he told her to look out the windows.

"I can see most of the floor from here, so if anything goes wrong, I know almost immediately, and we can come up with a plan of action."

She nodded, looking impressed, and Gabe swelled with pride. He didn't know what it was about her, but she made him feel like his life's mission was to impress her.

"This is incredible. I've never been in a glass or eyewear factory before." She turned to stare out the window again, and Gabe was entranced with her long dark hair. He hadn't seen it down like this since she'd worn it up the entire time at the ranch, but it hit around mid-back, and slight waves made him want to run his fingers through it.

Footsteps approached the door quickly, and Gabe knew it was Sophia from the rapid pace.

"Wow, what are you doing here so early? I thought you were going for a long run this morning." Sophia stood at the doorway, dressed in slacks and a nice blouse. Her hand sat on her hip, ready for an explanation.

Her voice caused Aubrey to turn around, and he could see

the red creep into her cheeks. She'd done that on more than one occasion since they'd met, and he still found it adorable every time.

"I found a friend along the way and decided to cut it short this morning. Sophia, this is Aubrey. Aubrey, my little sister, Sophia." He watched as Aubrey visibly relaxed after he'd mentioned sister.

"Aubrey Pearson? Here in Venice?" Sophia's mouth dropped open as she walked forward.

Aubrey took a few steps and reached out her hand, which Sophia crushed back into her body as she leaned in for the customary kisses on the cheek. Gabe tried to keep his smile to himself, but the corners seemed to be rebelling.

"I was surprised when Gabe mentioned you knew of me. It's been pretty nice for the past few years because all the media attention around my brothers' fame has died down, so I don't get recognized much anymore."

Sophia looked her up and down, and Gabe realized he was holding his breath. Having Sophia's good opinion of Aubrey meant more to him than he previously thought. But then again, he hadn't expected the American to show up in his country along his running route.

"You are beautiful. Your brothers are very attractive, but I think you won out on the looks, right, Gabe?" She turned a wicked grin in his direction.

"Absolutely." He stared into Aubrey's eyes, hoping to communicate his growing attraction for her.

Aubrey rolled her lips in and tucked a section of hair behind her ear, glancing down at the ground with some sort of anxiety.

"Let's not make her feel uncomfortable, Sof. She took the night train from Florence, so I'm sure she's tired." Gabe walked forward, and Sophia grinned at him.

"Are you kidding? I can't believe I'm actually meeting you.

Gabe was talking about you the other night at family dinner. He was saying—"

"It doesn't really matter, does it?" Gabe broke in, clapping his hands together firmly. "I'm just going to get a few things, and then I'm going to be Aubrey's tour guide for the day. Do you think you can handle things here?"

Sophia's eyes went wide, and she shook her hands as if she'd been holding something hot.

"You're going to let me take over the company for the day?" She sauntered over and sat in the chair behind Gabe's desk, resting her feet on top.

Gabe pushed them off. "Don't make me regret it. Don't sign anything or make any major decisions, and you'll be fine." He grabbed a sticky note and slipped it into his pocket. "Will you let Mom know we have a guest for dinner? And can you take her suitcase with you in the car? Then we won't be toting it all over the city."

Sophia pretended to look at an invisible watch on her wrist. "Sure. It's a good thing you thought of it now. She'll be wanting to make a feast when she finds out who it is." She giggled and smiled at Aubrey like she was a celebrity and Sophia was the fangirl. Aubrey had a hesitant smile on her face, and Gabe could feel the confusion and discomfort coming from her.

Grabbing her hand, he enjoyed the jolt of electricity running up his arm and pulled her out of the room before Sophia could say anything else. Once they were outside, he let her go and turned to her. "I'm sorry about her. She likes to talk a lot. She recently got back with her ex-boyfriend, and now she's just mush and roses."

That got Aubrey to laugh loud and deep. "And how do you really feel about it?"

"Eh, as long as I don't have to hear about him every time I'm in the room with her, I'm good with it." They walked a few steps, their hands swinging close with each step. "Where do you want to start?"

Aubrey pulled out a small note page from her purse and studied it for several seconds. "I researched a few places before I left home, but I think I'll take the native tour. You tell me. What do I need to see while here?" She stuffed the page back into her bag and looked up at him with a smile.

There were a few places he could take her, but there was one he really hoped she'd like. He'd start with some of the tourist spots and end with it.

CHAPTER 12

Gabe showed her several of the places around the factory and then took her back over to Venice on his boat. A few hours after they'd begun their tour, they stopped for some lunch at a small restaurant on Murano, the island just a short distance from Venice where the majority of the businesses on the island sold glass they'd blown right there for tourists to see. The entire experience had outshined her other days in Europe, as Gabe was well-versed in the history and a few jokes.

He'd caught her hand several times, and each time she felt as if fireworks had been lit inside her, the excitement almost uncontrollable. Things seemed so easy and carefree with him, even though she'd seen how tired he was in Utah, mostly from his work.

Live in the moment. That was all she could do right then. She didn't need to worry about what was going to happen a week from now, just that she was in a beautiful place with an attractive and fun guy at her side.

"How has Europe been so far? Is there anything you

haven't seen that you want to?" Gabe asked, taking a bite of his pasta with marinara.

Aubrey's cheeks still burned from when he had to whisper that there was no Alfredo sauce in Italy, as it had been made up by Americans. But her own pasta was heads and tails above the bottled stuff, so she was grateful for it.

"It's been really great, actually. But don't go getting a big head now," she said, trying to give him a serious look but failing as the corners of her mouth ticked upward. "I think I could watch those guys blow glass all day. That was fascinating."

Gabe smiled wide, sitting back in his chair. "I'm glad to hear it. I remember as a child that every Christmas, my mother would take us out there and let us pick an ornament for our tree. The talent they have for different figurines is amazing."

"That trumps the Pearson family tradition. We would just go to the store every year, or my Mom would pick one for us. I've got a box of them at home. She still picks them for us even though we're twenty-nine." Aubrey chuckled, and Gabe joined in, the deep sound of his laugh soothing something in her chest. "We did have the advantage of cutting down our own Christmas tree, though. The smell of pine through the house is something that can't be topped."

"What about the scented stuff? That makes it smell like Christmas to me." Gabe chuckled a bit. "We don't really have the advantage of mountains near our home, so we have to make do."

Aubrey thought about that for a moment. She'd only seen buildings and few plants and shrubs over near the factory. "You do what works, I guess. But the ranch is right next to the mountain, so it's almost mandatory." She smiled, twirling a forkful of pasta again.

"It's amazing what moms will do for their children. I

think you'll like my mom. She can seem a little overbearing at first, but once you give her a chance, she'd move the world for you if you asked."

"There's quite an age gap between you and Sophia. Did your mother have a hard time getting pregnant?" Aubrey asked it hesitantly, trying to gauge his reaction before she finished.

A sad smile crossed his face, and he nodded. "She had a few miscarriages after I was born, and for a while, she mourned that I wouldn't get to have any siblings. She comes from a big family and wanted several children running around the house." He paused a moment, his eyes faraway. "When Sophia made it safely, she was happier than I'd ever seen her. And Sophia definitely adds the right spice to our family."

Aubrey ate another bite of pasta, so many thoughts and questions moving through her head. She'd found an ease with Gabe that she hadn't felt with any guy she'd dated in her life, and he was like an open book. She had assumed at the ranch that he wasn't the family-man sort, but the way he was talking gave her hope that she'd been wrong.

"What about you? Do you plan to have kids in the future?" She couldn't meet his eyes, knowing her face would give away her embarrassment.

"I would love that. It's been hard to focus on my personal life the past few years with my father's health failing. That's why I'm the boss now. He had a heart attack, and the doctors say he's still too weak for a lot of stress. But ever since I got back from Utah, I've been trying to figure out a way to hire a few people to lighten my workload," he said, staring into her eyes and sending chills down her spine. "That's one of the reasons I hired Sophia. I don't want to be an absentee dad when the time comes, and I think that starts by preparing now."

Aubrey was grateful she was sitting down as she might have tripped and fallen if they were still walking the streets of Venice. That was an answer she hadn't expected from him, and her heart thumped wildly in her chest as she thought about it. All the American guys she'd dated had been so vague or had avoided her question about kids and a future, but Gabe had gone right for it. She hoped he wasn't just telling her what she wanted to hear.

Aubrey cleared her throat. "My parents were really good at that. Life at a working ranch with guests coming to see the experience can be somewhat hectic, but they always managed to take time out for us or would make sure we learned lessons as we mucked out stalls and moved hay. And their relationship, well, they still look at each other as though they've just met." She set her fork down and leaned back, glancing around the small restaurant, still in awe that she was actually here.

"That's important, I think." Gabe stood and walked over to pay the bill, giving Aubrey a few moments to collect herself.

She laughed at the assumptions she'd made about him just a couple weeks before. He was starting to sound a lot like someone she could spend her life with. But there was the little problem of them living thousands of miles apart. It didn't sound like he could just up and move to California or Aspen Hollow, which meant she'd have to leave everything she'd known and live here.

She put the brakes on those thoughts and shook her head. She was definitely going crazy. Gabe hadn't done anything to show he was feeling something more than just being a nice guy, beyond holding her hand. But it wasn't good to jump from that to marriage in a matter of days.

"Are you ready to go?" he asked, pulling his coat from the back of his chair.

Aubrey looked up, nodding. She stood, and he helped hold her coat while she slid her arms through. She felt like she was in an old-time movie and said, "Thank you," softly. With her heart galloping away, she was going to have to do something to protect herself. She wasn't sure what just yet, but she couldn't let her feelings get too far ahead, or she'd be nursing a broken heart when she made it back to the States.

As they walked out of the building, he slid his hand into hers, the action natural and without fanfare. She knew heartbreak would be in her future soon.

"**My** parents live just through here." Gabe placed his hand on the small of Aubrey's back as they walked through a garden area that was a small shortcut to his childhood home. The house was small and modest, but with most people living in small flats, it seemed like a palace while he was growing up.

Gabe hadn't been this nervous in quite some time, but just as he'd hoped Sophia approved of Aubrey when they were at the office, he hoped his parents would as well. It had been a while since he'd felt attracted to someone, and for some reason, he really hoped that their approval of her might be a sign that maybe he could get a new start with his future. Not that it would be easy with them living on different continents, but it was still early.

Once inside the door, he helped her remove her coat and then took his own off and moved them to one of the bedrooms. He hurried back, hoping she didn't feel lost or like he'd abandoned her in a strange place.

"This room is beautiful." Aubrey's face showed wonder as she looked around at the many things his mother had collected over the years. She loved little figurines and glass plates, and her finds were displayed throughout the room.

"Thank you. It's looked like this since I was young. There have been a few broken pieces here and there, but most of it survived two rambunctious kids." He chuckled a bit, and she joined in, the sound making this the most right thing in his life. He really liked this girl, and while it had been chance that they'd seen each other that morning on the pier, he somehow wished it could be more long-term than just two days.

Standing in front of several of the small pieces near the fireplace, Aubrey leaned forward to inspect them. Gabe moved up behind her, breathing in that vanilla scent and running his fingers through the bottom section of her hair. She turned, smiling at him.

"Your hair is very soft." He grimaced, immediately wishing he'd kept that comment to himself.

"Thank you. It's not often I get someone willing to comb through it for me." She grinned at him, her blue eyes twinkling in the dim light of the overhead fixture.

"Gabe? Is that you?" his mother called out, pulling him from his trance.

"Yes, Mom. We're in the living room." He heard steps on the stairs and moved in that direction, motioning for Aubrey to follow him. He whispered in her ear right before they made it to the door, "She'll greet you with two kisses, starting on the right side."

Aubrey frowned. "I wish you'd told me that before your sister showed up." One corner of her mouth tilted up, and Gabe grinned at her.

They walked into the kitchen, and his mother turned from mixing the insalata in a bowl on the counter. When she glanced up, she smiled wide.

"This is our guest? She is beautiful." She moved around

the counter and gave Aubrey the customary greeting, which Aubrey accepted with ease this time. The slight brokenness of her English was something Gabe was proud of, as his stubborn mother had taken a long time to come around to the idea of learning another language. But when Gabe had so many American friends after college, she'd begun to learn slowly. "It's so nice you here. I am Amara and my husband is, Giovanni. He'll be back in a few minutes."

"Thank you for allowing me to stay the night. I could use a real bed instead of the night trains."

"Sophia tells me you are the sister to the Pearsons. It's so nice to finally meet you. Gabe was telling us you were at the ranch—"

"Is there something I can help you with, Mom?" Gabe took in a deep breath, hoping to change the direction of the conversation. He couldn't remember what all he'd said about Aubrey that night he'd arrived home, but he didn't want her to think he was some creep, talking about her as though she were more than a casual acquaintance.

His mother paused and gave him a look. He tried to make a silent plea for her to drop the subject, and after several seconds of suspense, she nodded. "Will you set the table? Your father should be home with Sophia soon." She gave him a quick wink and moved back to the stove.

"Can I help you cook or chop anything?" Aubrey asked, moving toward his mother.

With a wide grin on her face, she said, "That would be lovely, my dear. Will you just cut those tomatoes for the salad?"

Aubrey's head was bent as she began the task, and his mom looked up at Gabe and gave him a quick nod. It was similar to her approval of Nicoletta all those years ago, and excitement burst through his chest. He hadn't felt like this in so long, and it was refreshing to like someone with all the qualities Aubrey had.

He just hoped they could enjoy the dinner and have a good evening. She'd probably leave tomorrow afternoon, and a part of him mourned her quick departure even with several hours to go. He didn't know what to do about it just yet, but he hoped she'd give him a sign of her feelings. He'd find a way to make anything work, as she was becoming someone he couldn't part with forever.

Aubrey cut several tomatoes and other veggies for the dinner, and within about fifteen minutes of their arrival, Gabe's father and sister arrived, just in time for the meal to begin.

Gabe made the introductions between her and her father, and Sophia walked up and kissed both cheeks again in greeting. Aubrey felt like she was getting the hang of it finally. She just wished Gabe had warned her before the whole awkward encounter at the office.

"What is it you do in California, Aubrey?" Gabe's father, Giovanni, asked. His English was very good, almost as good as Gabe's.

"I am a labor and delivery nurse. I check vitals and help assist with the delivery and care of new babies and their mothers." Aubrey smiled, remembering some of the little babies she'd helped deliver before coming on her trip. There had been some scary instances, but for the most part, the babies were healthy and headed home in a day or two. It sounded like a mantra in her life. Even the mom with triplets had delivered all three safely, and all of them were thriving in the NICU.

"That's amazing, getting to hold all those little babies," Sophia said, her face beaming with excitement. "How long have you been doing that?"

"In Labor and Delivery? About two and a half years. I was in the emergency department before that. Working with pregnant women is a lot easier than some of the things that come through the emergency doors." There were several memories that she did her best to block out because of being hit or kicked. Then others when the case was so sad that it nearly broke her heart to hear about.

"I was able to witness her abilities firsthand at the reunion when one of the guys fell off a horse. It was pretty impressive." Gabe smiled and winked at her. "Why did you become a nurse?" he asked. He looked just as entranced with her career as the rest of the family, and for once, she realized how grateful she was for the skills she'd learned while taking care of people. Not everyone got to see some of the miracles she'd seen happen. She'd just been too frustrated and full of self-pity to see it.

Smiling, Aubrey set her fork down next to her plate and folded her arms on the edge of the table. "When I was about seven, I was playing outside with my best friend, Sadie, who is now my sister-in-law, by the way. She married Evan. We started hearing this small cry and went searching to find where it was coming from. A small cat had gotten its leg stuck in some wire back in the trees. It took some coaxing to get it to calm down, but we got her free. I took her inside, trying to figure out how to help the gash in her leg.

"My mom came in and saw me with a cat and the box of bandages and ointment, ready to take care of it like I would a cut. She took me and the cat into the vet, and I was mesmerized by all that the vet did to take care of the animal."

"So, why not a vet?" Sophia asked.

"I was just drawn to helping people. Taking care of animals is what we did on the ranch every day, and it's kind of like therapy after some time away. Working with the animals in a non-medical way is soothing for me, and I never get sick of it."

Gabe looked at her with concern, his eyebrows cinched together as his jaw worked back and forth. "Are you sick of your job?"

Aubrey glanced at all the eyes watching her, feeling self-conscious all of a sudden. "No, I think I just needed this break. Something to put life into perspective, you know?"

"That's what Gabe said about the trip to your ranch. I think it helped him in more ways than one." Amara grinned and stood to grab the dessert.

"Signore Alessandro, how did you get into the eyewear business?" Aubrey asked, hoping to deflect some of the attention for a bit.

The older version of Gabe smiled, the wrinkles around his eyes making it hard to see where he was looking. "My father started it after the last war. It's a business that has evolved quite a bit over the last few decades, but I'm sure he would be proud of where Gabe has led the company."

He gave his son a warm smile and a quick nod, causing Gabe to sit up a bit straighter.

When everything was cleaned up, it was nearly nine in the evening, and Aubrey felt the exhaustion down to her bones.

Gabe leaned against the doorframe that led into the room she would be sleeping in for the night. "What time will you be leaving tomorrow?"

Aubrey paused for several seconds, not sure how to answer that. "I'm not really sure. I had such a great time today that I haven't checked any train or bus schedules."

A look of relief passed over his face before he smiled. "Are you up for an early morning adventure?"

"How early are we talking?" Aubrey asked. She wasn't sure she could get up before noon after all the traveling she'd done.

"I'll come pick you up around 6:45 am. There's something I want you to see before you leave Venice." He gave her a hesitant smile and then asked, "Where are you headed to next?"

"My plan was to head up north and go skiing. It's been a while since I've been, and I figured why not try it out here?"

Gabe glanced at her small suitcase. "Do you have mini snow clothes in that bag?" He chuckled, and Aubrey joined in.

"No, I hadn't thought about that. Maybe I'll find somewhere else to go instead."

"Sophia has a bunch of stuff, and you look like you're about the same size. I'm sure she'd let you borrow it."

Aubrey shook her head. "I couldn't borrow it from her. How would I get it back?" She studied Gabe's face, enjoying the way he bit his lip as he thought about it.

After almost a minute of silence, he snapped his fingers and said, "Would you be willing to have a tour guide for a bit longer?"

Tilting her head to the side, Aubrey narrowed her eyes. "How do you mean?"

"I mean, what if I drive you up there? It's been a while since I've been skiing, and I could use a good excuse to go. That way you don't have to make ten connections to get there, and then I can bring Sophia's snow stuff back to her."

Aubrey smiled, and her insides bubbled with excitement. She wouldn't have to say goodbye to him just yet. Although, would the extra time cause her attachment to him to grow stronger? Her mouth spoke before her mind came to a conclusion. "I think that sounds like a great plan. Will your work be okay with you gone for a couple days?"

"I'm sure Sophia will be ecstatic. And my father can help her with anything major. I just need to meet with one client tomorrow, and then we can head out. But I'll still pick you up in the morning first." He gave her that lopsided grin she was coming to adore, and she nodded, biting her bottom lip.

An attractive, kind Italian guy asking her to go on a morning excursion some would call a date? How could she refuse?

Her alarm clock rang earlier than Aubrey thought possible. She'd gone to bed soon after Gabe left to go home, but her exhausted body couldn't convince her brain to slow down. She'd gone over just about every minute of their tour through Venice and hadn't fallen asleep until close to two in the morning.

After turning off her phone alarm, she slipped out of bed and changed her clothes, trying to be quiet as she didn't know the schedule of the rest of the family. After freshening up in the bathroom, she pulled half of her hair back and grabbed her purse and coat, not sure what exactly she'd need on this excursion. She crept out of her room and opened the front door slowly, hoping to let everyone sleep longer.

She turned around to find Gabe standing next to her in the dark. Crying out and jumping back, she said, "You scared me!"

Gabe held up one hand and then rested it on her shoulder, his touch sending her mind into overload. "I'm sorry," he whispered. "I was going to say something, but I figured I was going to scare you no matter what happened."

"You're probably right. At least I'm fully awake now."

They made small talk as they made their way to the docks and got into his boat once again. When they were back near the square where they'd bumped into each other the day before, he docked the boat. He grabbed a large bag from the back seat and slung it across his body before walking onto the dock.

Aubrey looked at the bag and wondered what that could mean. "We're not going scuba diving or anything, right?"

He looked down at the bag. "Uh, no. This is just for where we're going." He helped her out of the boat and stepped back. Something about him seemed nervous, like he wasn't sure what to do with his hands, and he finally stuffed them into his coat pockets.

The large tower in the square called San Marco Campanile had captured her attention yesterday when Gabe had told her that it collapsed at the beginning of the twentieth century. It was beautiful, and she was grateful they'd rebuilt it.

Once at the bottom of the tower, Aubrey saw a man dressed in what looked like a maintenance uniform. Gabe spoke in Italian, and she could understand a few words here and there as it was similar to Spanish. She'd gotten a minor in Spanish at Hawthorne and was grateful she'd spent the time to learn it.

"Okay, are you ready?" Gabe asked, taking her hand. She loved the feel of her hand in his, the warmth and strength of his hands making her feel safe, even though there wasn't much to worry about in a tower.

The man had opened the door, and Gabe led her toward it. "Are we going up the tower?" She hadn't felt this amount of excitement, well, since the day before, and she couldn't believe he'd arranged for this to happen.

Before they made it to the very top, Gabe stepped behind

her, placing his hand over her eyes. "Just take a few steps up, and we'll be at the top. Good, okay, stop right there. Keep your eyes closed." He held onto her once they stopped and pulled his hand away from her face. "Okay, open your eyes."

She did as instructed and was struck by the beauty around her. The tower loomed over most of Venice, allowing her to see all around. The sun was just coming over the horizon, and as it reflected over the water, she was sure she could die happy right then.

"I can't believe you arranged all this. Thank you. This is… beautiful." She put her hand over her mouth and leaned back into him, overwhelmed that he would take the time to do something as magnificent as this for her. He pulled her in, wrapping both arms around her upper body. She'd never felt more comfortable than she did at that moment.

They stood there for several minutes in silence, enjoying the beauty of the rising sun. Gabe eventually moved away, saying something about having to get the rest of the surprise ready.

Taking a few steps toward the opening of the tower, she pulled out her phone and took several pictures of the surrounding area. She frowned a bit when she saw they didn't do the scene justice. She heard rustling behind her, but she was so captivated by the landscape that she didn't register what was happening until she felt Gabe's arm slide around her shoulder, pulling her to his side.

Aubrey leaned her head against his shoulder, feeling more comfortable than she had in a while. Sure, him holding her like this would usually make her run for the hills if she'd only known someone as long as they'd known each other, but for some reason, she felt at peace.

"This is amazing. Everything is so breathtaking," she said, turning to face him. She gasped at their close proximity but quickly recovered by saying, "Thank you for bringing me up here. This is something I'll never forget."

Gabe smiled, his chestnut eyes boring into hers. "I, uh, brought some food for breakfast. I wasn't sure what you liked exactly, but take your pick." He didn't look away from her, and she could tell his breathing had increased, causing her to smile. At least she wasn't the only one feeling a little breathless all of a sudden.

Aubrey looked between the small picnic and Gabe and felt something connect between them. If something didn't come of the two of them, she'd be ruined for all guys ever. Why didn't anyone tell her Italian guys were the way to go?

She sat on the small blanket he'd set out and pulled a croissant from the pile.

He picked up a coffee cup and handed it to her. "I wasn't sure if you are a coffee drinker, but I know your brothers like hot chocolate, so I thought I'd get that for you."

"Thank you. For all this. What time did you get up this morning?" Aubrey asked, sipping the warm liquid. It wasn't quite as sweet as she was used to, but it was warm, and with the cool air blowing through, she could use the heat.

He took a seat next to her, sitting only an inch or two away, and gave her a sheepish look. "Earlier than I should have." He took off the lid of his cup and dunked a piece of biscotti into it. "So, now my question is, which city in Europe has been your favorite so far?"

Aubrey couldn't help but grin, and she shook her head. "It's no contest after all this. Definitely Venice."

"I'll call this a win, then." Gabe smiled at her, causing her insides to do somersaults. They sat in silence for a while longer, enjoying the beautiful sunrise and the light breakfast Gabe had prepared.

When they were done eating, she lifted her phone in front

of them and said, "Say cheese!" With their cheeks touching, Aubrey smiled wide, loving the smile of the guy in the frame with her. Such a perfect moment she wanted to keep it fresh in her mind forever.

The smell of his cologne wafted to her nose, and she turned to look at him, wondering if he was for real. She was glad he was coming with her to go skiing, because after this moment, she wasn't sure she could say goodbye without tears.

He must have felt her staring at him, because he turned to look at her, his eyes searching her face. She wasn't sure how long they looked at each other like that, but her heart leaped as he inched forward, their breath mingling together. She closed her eyes, waiting for his lips to touch hers. But before it happened, a voice called out behind them.

"Signore Alessandro, it's time."

Gabe pulled away and acknowledged the man. "Thank you. We'll pack up and head down." He looked back at Aubrey and gave her a sad smile. "Sorry, we have to head back down before the square gets busy. Not everyone is allowed up here."

She could tell he didn't say it to brag or throw his wealth in her face, but she wished that the guard could have given them one more minute. Or two. Now the moment was broken, and she hoped that wasn't the last one they would have together.

After another minute or two of packing up the food, they began the descent, the only sound their shoes on the stone steps.

Once they were back outside, Aubrey hooked her arm through his and leaned her head against his shoulder. The morning had been so perfect, and she was pretty sure she'd never felt this deeply for anyone ever. But things were moving so fast. Was it going to end up just like her other relationships because they lived so far apart?

Pushing those thoughts away, she focused on getting back into the boat. For once, she was going to see how things played out over the next forty-eight hours before jumping to conclusions and fantasies.

The morning had gone off almost without a hitch, and he'd loved spending time with Aubrey, though he wished they could have kissed at the top of the tower. That would have been the most romantic story ever, but maybe it was better that they'd had to go.

As he thought more about it, a picture of Nicoletta popped into his head, causing a rising guilt to form in his throat. It had been so long since her passing, and he'd changed a lot since then. Would they have been a good couple over the past decade if she'd not gotten cancer and died? Even still, the thought that he should be happy without her caused him to push the thoughts out of his mind. He had work to do, and for the first time in quite a while, he was having fun being with Aubrey. However long that would last, he didn't know, but this was one situation he felt would be better if he didn't overanalyze and just went with it.

He'd dropped Aubrey off at his parents' home and told her he'd meet up after his meeting, hoping things would be quick so they could start the journey before a crazy amount of traffic formed.

Walking into the office, he organized a few papers on his desk, trying to put things back together from when Sophia had taken over the day before. He'd forgotten to note who he was meeting with today, only that it was important. Now it was a short meeting standing in the way of a fun little vacation with Aubrey.

A few minutes later, there was a short knock on the door, and he said, "Come in," sliding the last sheet of paper into a report he needed to look at next week.

The door creaked open, and he heard steps coming in his direction. Looking up, he felt the blood drain from his face. The man standing before him was Signore Bianchi, Nicoletta's father.

"Signore Bianchi, what a surprise. Is there something I can help you with, sir?" Gabe stood, reaching his hand across the desk to shake. The man shook it and took a seat.

He stretched out his hands and said, "Surprise? We booked this meeting a couple of weeks ago."

Nodding, Gabe sat and said, "I know, but after our phone call, I must have forgotten to put more than the appointment time for this meeting, and a lot has happened since then. It's good to see you, sir. How have things been?" Gabe swallowed hard, feeling like he was back in grade school about to receive a reprimand from one of his teachers. Signore Bianchi had always been strict on the rules of seeing Nicoletta, his large stature providing the necessary intimidation for Gabe to be worried every time he came around.

"Things are better, much better. Thank you. Matteo just finished university, and my wife has been busy with the charity. You knew we put together a charity in Nicoletta's name, right?"

"My mother might have mentioned it at one point, sir. Will you add us to your list of donors?" Gabe worked to keep his emotions in check, knowing that money wouldn't help her now. But it could help with future cures, and he wanted to help, if only to save someone from the struggles he'd gone through for so long after her passing.

Signore Bianchi smiled. "We would appreciate that. There is an experimental treatment right now that they are hoping will show signs of killing the cancer Nicoletta had." He placed his fingers at his mouth and tapped a few times before moving them back to his lap. "She always did love you, you know? Everything was about you or memories you two had together. I just wish I'd been there more earlier on."

Gabe could see the tears form in the man's eyes, and his heart went out to him. "She's always been special to me." He hesitated a moment, feeling thrown off of his usual authoritative stand in meetings such as these. "Is there something else I can do for you, sir?"

"Yes, I work for Giordano Eyewear now. I was to come negotiate some of the final terms of the new contract if you have time." He must have caught Gabe looking at his watch.

"Of course, I have some time for an old friend. Let me get the contract printed out for both of us, and we can go over the changes you need to make. Can I get you anything? Tea? Coffee?"

Signore Bianchi shook his head. "I'm fine for now. Let's go through this."

Blowing out a long breath, he knew this wasn't going to be a quick meeting like he'd planned.

I hope to be back before lunch so we can take off. I'll hurry as fast as I can. Gabe

He felt the guilt as he sent the message to Aubrey, wishing he could have canceled this meeting before it began. But he would make sure to leave as soon as negotiations wrapped up. He wasn't about to miss another minute with the girl he was falling for because of work.

CHAPTER 17

The hours ticked by, and Aubrey was beginning to wonder if Gabe had been kidnapped on his way to his parents' home. Amara, his mother, had taken her out to the market and to run a few errands, and each time she stopped to talk to someone, Aubrey wanted to hurry it along so she could be there when Gabe came to pick her up. At least he'd texted her about the meeting taking longer.

"It sounds like Gabe is in a meeting with Signore Bianchi," Amara said, turning away from the friend she'd been talking to. "My friend saw Signore on the way over and said he was heading into Cristallo."

Puzzled, Aubrey tried to remember if they'd discussed a Signore Bianchi ever but couldn't understand why that would be a big deal.

Amara saw the look and patted her arm. "Signore Bianchi is the father of Gabe's childhood sweetheart. They had done everything together from the time they were small until she passed away from a rare form of cancer during the Christmas holidays of Gabe's first year of college. It took quite a few years for Gabe to recover from the shock of it all, and there are days when I'm still grateful for people like your brothers and the rest of the little club they have together. I don't think Gabe would be the man he is today if they hadn't been there for him."

As the details started clicking together, a vague memory surfaced where Aiden had told her about one of his frat brothers losing his girlfriend to cancer. Something about her throwing him for a loop by her knowing about it for months but not telling him until the week before she died.

"Why would Signore Bianchi want to meet with Gabe?"

"I'm not sure, but it will be interesting to see what happens. The Bianchis moved to Verona shortly after Nicoletta died, and I don't think Gabe has seen the family for nearly twelve years."

A pit formed in Aubrey's stomach, worry at what this meeting might trigger and if maybe it would be better for her to head out now, on her own. She'd never lost someone that close to her, but she'd seen the mess Sadie'd had to live through, the memories that triggered so much sadness.

But Aubrey was used to listening to people in pain or those who were just biding time until delivery and wanted to talk. It was the least she could do for Gabe after all he'd done over the past two days. Whether she left Europe with another friend or someone worth holding on to was yet to be determined, but she hoped they could work through whatever he needed with the time they had together.

Well after eight in the evening, Gabe walked into the house. He came over to the table where Aubrey and the other three Alessandros had begun eating dinner. "I'm so sorry I'm late, everyone." Looking straight at Aubrey, he asked, "Do you want to head out now? Or eat and then go? I think some of the traffic might be gone in the next hour, so that might free up the highways for a quicker drive."

The look on his face made Aubrey want to gather him in

her arms and hold on to him for as long as it took for him to feel better.

"Let's eat. I can use one more of your mother's dinners as a reminder of my time here." She smiled wide at Gabe, trying to convey that she understood. Reacting on her instinct, she pulled him to her, giving him a long, tight hug. She just hoped they were at a point where they could confide in each other, or it would be a long ride to Northern Italy.

CHAPTER 18

At nearly ten on Friday night, they loaded up snow clothes and a few snacks his mother had organized for them and got into Gabe's car, ready to make the three-and-a-half-hour drive north.

They talked about little stuff here and there while navigating the roads, and Aubrey played with the radio, trying to find something to listen to. Gabe grinned at her, knowing it wasn't going to be as easy as where she was from to find something she wanted to listen to.

When she sat back, she rested her arm on the console, and after several seconds of indecision, Gabe slipped his hand into hers, enjoying the softness of her skin and how well their hands fit together. He tried to keep his eyes forward, but he loved seeing her light up with a smile.

"How did your meeting go today?" she asked, turning in her seat to face him.

Several emotions coursed through him as he remembered his time with Signore Bianchi. "It was okay. Just some negotiations of a contract with a company we've been trying to work out a contract with." He looked at her with a frown.

"I'm really so sorry about the delay. I usually know exactly who I'm meeting with and why, but I forgot to write it down before I left for Utah. Otherwise, I would have canceled so I could be with you."

"Gabe, it's fine. I understand. But now I know why you need to hire some more people. I get tired enough having to work a twelve-hour night shift a couple of times a week. But if you're constantly negotiating contracts for hours on end, that would be rough."

Squeezing her hand a bit, he was grateful she understood. And she was right. He needed to make finding help his main goal after this ski trip. He deserved to have a life just like his own workers who went home after their shift and didn't have to worry about what would happen the next day.

It was her next question that threw him off. "Your mother told me the man you met with is the father of Nicoletta. I remember Evan and Aiden talking about how hard her death hit you. I can imagine it was hard to see him after all these years."

Gabe didn't know why he was surprised that his mother knew about his meeting with Nicoletta's father, but the fact that Aubrey already knew something about it seemed to ease a measure of guilt in his chest.

"It was a shock, but we talked a bit and then got to business."

"Was it really hard after she died?"

Swallowing back the mound that was forming in his throat, Gabe wondered how he could change the conversation. He pulled his hand away from hers to take a drink from the bottle of water and focused on the road.

"To be honest, for a few months, I wished I had died in her place. She'd always been there to encourage me, to laugh at my lame jokes. It was hard for a while, but with college and then work, I didn't have much time to think about it after a while." He took in a deep breath, surprised at how easy it was to talk about it.

"When I came home after graduation is when it hit me the most. Being back in Venice all the time except for the short breaks was hard, as I had so many memories from our time together. But time eased the ache, and now I've been able to look at them as good memories of a great childhood. I just hope my mom will stop setting me up on dates now."

Aubrey laughed, and Gabe wasn't quite sure how to take it. He glanced at her before looking back at the road.

"I'm sorry. I told you my mom has tried to set me up on dates. It must be a mother thing to do, no matter the culture." Her wide smile showed her straight white teeth. After a few seconds, her face turned somber. "What do you mean 'stop now'?"

Gabe glanced at her for several seconds. "I like you, Aubrey. There is so much to you, and I love discovering every bit."

"I might like you a little bit too," Aubrey said, biting her lip and looking out the windshield.

The rest of the drive was more relaxed, although a nugget of guilt sat in his stomach. Signore Bianchi's words that Nicoletta cared for him burned. Was he betraying what he'd had with Nicoletta so long ago by the feelings building inside him for Aubrey? He was entitled to a happily ever after, wasn't he?

The more he thought about that, the more he realized it was true. Nicoletta would always be his first love and first heartbreak, but it had been long enough. He deserved someone with whom he could share his life and share part of the burden of the company with instead of shouldering it all himself. And it would be nice to have an excuse for adventures like this more often.

As they drove into the parking lot for the Hotels and

Chalets Edelweiss, Aubrey pulled out a paper from her bag on the floor and searched for something.

"Do you mind dropping me off at this hotel?" She moved the paper over with her thumb next to the name and then pointed to the ones sitting in front of them. "These are out of my price range."

Gabe looked at her with a straight face, the emotions tumbling through him. It had been a while since someone hadn't just expected him to pay for everything. He shook his head. "No, don't worry about it. This is my treat."

"Really, you don't have to. I had planned to stay at one of the smaller hotels anyway."

Reaching over, Gabe took her hand in his. "Please, let me do this. I'm the one who invited myself along on this excursion."

She looked down and blew out a breath. "I just feel bad. I've seen people take advantage of my brothers, and I can only imagine your life is the same too." She dug into her purse once more and pulled out several euros. "Here, please take this."

Gabe sat back with his hands in front of him. "No, save it for the next part of your trip." He hurried and opened the door, stepping out before she could stick the papers into his pocket. "I'll go in and see about getting us two rooms," he said, grinning at her through the window.

She nodded, rolling her eyes as she put the money back into her bag. Just one more reason he liked this girl. She didn't care about his money, but she seemed to like spending time with him, which was a plus. And she'd said she liked him. He just hoped they could make something work after she moved on to the next destination on her European tour.

CHAPTER 19

They drove from their hotel into Val Senales Glacier Ski Resort and parked at the base of the mountains early Saturday morning. Aubrey held the cup of hot chocolate Gabe had brought to her door that morning, grateful for the warmth on her hands. The weather outside was cold, and she could imagine it would be even worse on top of the slopes.

Aubrey leaned forward to look at the resort through the windshield. "Wow, I didn't expect them to be so steep." She gulped. It had been a long time since she'd gone skiing, between being so busy at work and living by the beach. She hoped it was like getting back on a horse.

"You'll get the hang of it. There are a lot of smaller hills we'll take to get you feeling more comfortable." He grinned and opened the car door. More comfortable? She'd never done anything more than the bunny hills at home. "Then we can race down the bigger hills."

She hadn't seen that competitive spirit come out since their card games on the ranch, but if he was going to race, she wasn't going to let him win every time. With a chuckle, she got out of the car and helped pull out their gear from the trunk. They dressed in snow pants, coats, gloves, scarves, hats, goggles, and ski boots.

"Wow, I'm actually surprised how well these fit," Aubrey said, zipping up the coat. It felt like she was wearing her own snow clothes, and even the ski boots had a few centimeters of wiggle room.

"Good guess on my part," Gabe said, grinning. "Let's get started." They walked up to the window to buy lift passes and rent two sets of skis with poles.

As they waited for the attendant to get their skis, Aubrey turned to look at Gabe, a small smirk on her face. "I'm surprised you don't own a pair of high-end skis."

Gabe turned to look at her, his eyes searching her face. When she couldn't hold back the smile anymore, he laughed, tipping his head back in the process. "Most people think I own everything because of my bank account. But to be honest, it's been a while since I've been skiing. I can just hear my mother now. 'Gabriele Giovanni Alessandro, why are we storing skis you never use?'"

The higher-pitched tone he used to sound like his mother had Aubrey doubled over with laughter. The funny thing was, she could picture Amara saying something like that.

"It's good to know how similar our moms are. My mom is constantly asking when she can empty out my room so she can turn it into a gym or studio. But it's nice to come home to a place that's comforting. Like a haven." Something twisted in Aubrey's gut. This was the first time she'd realized how much she'd hung on to the past. She didn't want to move out completely because what if things didn't work out and there was no longer a place for her?

Gabe only nodded and handed her the skis from the

attendant. The thoughts stayed with her for several minutes as they waited for the gondola to take them up to the top of the slopes. Was that the reason her relationships never lasted? Because she didn't jump in with both feet?

"Already cold?" Gabe asked, and Aubrey realized she was moving from one foot to the other, her breath visible in the air. When she nodded, he stepped closer, holding his gear in one hand and wrapping his other arm around her, pulling her in close.

She couldn't put her finger on the smell of cologne he wore, but it was fresh, like the ocean. Fitting for the man that spent his days traveling back and forth to his home on an island. She was grateful for the warmth of his body next to hers, but it still took another minute for the chills to stop.

The gondola came, and they climbed in with a handful of other skiers, many of them speaking in different languages. She loved listening to the conversations and watching the facial expressions of people from all over the world.

"Euro for your thoughts?" Gabe said, resting his arm on the back of Aubrey's chair, his finger twirling at the hair at the end of her braid.

"Good one," Aubrey said, grinning.

"I picked up a few American phrases when I went to college. I figured I'd change it up a bit for you since you're here." He smiled, but something in his eyes looked distant, and she wondered what he was thinking about.

Aubrey pointed to the group of people sitting on a bench in front of them. "I just like watching people. I learned it from my dad. He'd take us to the fountain in the middle of Aspen Hollow, and we'd just watch people run around doing different things. He could usually call where the person was off to before asking them."

The gondola stopped before he said anything, and they

stood, moving to the doors at the back of the crowd. The two of them found an outside bench for putting their skis on and then headed for the first hill. Aubrey's stomach flipped as she watched Gabe move in front of her with ease, his agile body looking like he skied every day of his life.

Nerves welled up inside her, and she moved her poles only a few inches, making sure her start was slow and steady. There was something about sliding down a hill with two pieces of wood that was both exhilarating and terrifying at the same time.

She'd go a few feet and then put her legs together in what her father had called the snowplow, basically bringing the fronts of the skis together in a V shape. It would slow her down enough to give her control, enough that she didn't freeze up and sit down where she was.

By the time she made it down to Gabe, he gave her a look to suggest he'd been worried. "Are you all right? I was beginning to wonder if you'd fallen and I just left you there."

Aubrey shook her head. "No, I stood up the entire way down, which is always good." She grinned at him. "I told you, it's been a while. And I've worked in the emergency room when skiers have come in with injuries, so I'm hoping to avoid any of that."

"I guess I can understand that." Gabe looked as though he wanted to say something else but refrained. "Just let me know when you're ready to race. It will help you feel better after losing to me at cards so many times."

Aubrey slugged him in the shoulder, but the action did nothing to change the thousand-watt smile on his face.

"Of course you would make this a competition," she said, biting the inside of her cheek. "Okay, give me three more runs down this hill, and I'll race you."

"Deal." Gabe nodded and moved alongside her to the lift.

She'd been shaky enough going down that first time that a few more times wasn't going to make her comfortable with the mountain. But he'd sparked that competitiveness in her as well, and she wasn't about to back down from the challenge.

CHAPTER 20

After several hours and a stop for lunch at the little restaurant on the hill, Gabe was glad he'd come as he hadn't been able to do this in a long time. Every once in a while, memories of Nicoletta would pop up, as they'd spent a lot of time skiing during their teenage years.

They'd raced down the slower hill three times in a row, with Aubrey beating him two of the times. He wasn't sure what had gotten into her, but the adrenaline was flowing through him now, and he was ready for another shot at a win.

"Should we try another hill?" he asked, looking toward the ones that were a bit more challenging. The need to go fast was overwhelming him.

"You go ahead on that one over there. I'll meet you when I make it down this hill again." Aubrey gave him a half-smile, and part of him wondered if she could feel his impatience.

"You don't mind?"

She rolled her eyes. "Gabe, I just need to get one more under my belt before we go for the Black Diamond slopes."

He grinned at her. "That's not a Black Diamond. It's more

like a moderately hard slope. I'll wait for you here, and then we'll go over there."

She bit her lip and glanced up at the other slope, the nerves showing on her face. "You go, and I'll meet you over there after this run."

She turned to go back up the lift for the hills they'd been on, and Gabe watched her go, debating internally whether or not it was selfish to go on one of the steeper slopes. He just needed something to keep his mind from remembering things, to focus on the fact that he could be happy now, and with Aubrey. She'd admitted she had feelings for him, and he hoped there could be something more lasting than a three-day adventure in his country.

The minute he stepped off the lift to the new slope, he knew he'd needed this. The wind whipped past his face, and he moved back and forth across the hill, whipping in and out of trees as though he were competing at the Olympics. By the time he made it to the bottom of the hill, he raised his poles in the air with a feeling of triumph, the scene fading before his eyes.

He moved over to watch the hill Aubrey would be coming down and was surprised to find the girl in the purple coat moving at a much faster speed than she had the last few times.

When she reached the bottom, she pulled her goggles up, grinning from ear to ear. "It's kind of fun going fast." The twinkle in Aubrey's eyes made him match her smile.

"Do you want to try this other hill with me? It wasn't much different aside from a few trees in the course." He rolled his lips in and tried to give her the look of a puppy dog.

Her jaw twitched back and forth before she said, "I'll try it, I guess. It's not like I'm in Italy every day. And it would be nice to beat you once more." She strode past him, and Gabe chuckled, liking the competitive spirit she brought.

Once they got to the top of the hill, Aubrey took his hand and squeezed it, leaning her head on his shoulder. After a few seconds, she looked down the slope and then back up to him, her eyes wide with terror.

"Not much different? Do you see those narrow areas?" She pointed to them and then looked back at him, nearly shaking.

Gabe put a hand on each of her shoulders, rubbing them up and down in the hopes that it would reassure her. "You will do great. You've been doing amazing anyway. I just watched that last run on the other hill, and I was surprised at how easy you made it look."

"This is a new hill, though. That other one didn't have any obstacles I could ski right into."

"Okay, let's do a practice run. Just ski right behind me, and we won't worry about racing for another couple of runs." He watched as some of the panic seeped out of her, her face softening and drawing him in as she nodded.

They locked eyes again, and Gabe leaned forward, knowing it wasn't the perfect moment for a first kiss, but he couldn't resist any longer.

His lips touched hers, and heat flooded his chilled body. She wrapped her arms around his neck and pulled him down another inch, kissing him back with a passion that surprised him. After several seconds, she pulled away, breathless.

He waited, looking into her eyes and trying to read her expression. "A kiss for good luck," he finally said, a wide grin spreading across his face.

Aubrey leaned up and gave him a quick peck on the lips again. "Two kisses."

At that point, Gabe was ready to abandon skiing and continue kissing, but Aubrey grinned before pushing off the top of the slope, heading down the hill with confidence. Gabe shook his head, laughing that she'd thrown him off guard, and rushed to catch up to her.

He moved next to her, grinning at her look of frustration with him catching up so quickly. He moved out in front, gaining speed as he did so. She was several meters back now, and Gabe turned forward in time to miss a tree and a large boulder which looked like many of the skiers used as a jump. He just hoped Aubrey would avoid both. Coming to a stop several meters later, he turned back to see if he could warn her.

She was clear of the tree and almost the rock, but her right ski hit the edge of it, sending her flying through the air. It seemed as if time had slowed down as he watched her flip and turn, her body tense as if trying to brace herself for impact. Once she hit the snow, Gabe could hear a pop, but he wasn't sure what it was at first.

He unhooked his skis and trudged up the hill as fast as he could go. He knelt beside her. "Aubrey, are you all right? What can I do?" He watched her face scrunch together in pain for several seconds before she opened her eyes.

"It's my knee. I heard something pop when I landed." She moved to her elbows, biting her lip as she did so. "And I think I sprained my wrist. Is there a number to call for emergencies here? If not, will you ski down and get them? I don't think I'll be able to make it down the hill on my own."

"I left my phone in the car, but I'll go get help. What can I do for you until I get back?" Gabe looked around them, seeing only snow, the large rock several feet up, and a few trees scattered here and there.

Aubrey shook her head. "No, I should be fine. I think it's my ACL or MCL, and it will be better to just hang out here than try to ski on it again."

Gabe leaned forward, kissing her forehead before he ran

down and hooked his skis back on. The trail had lost its appeal, and the guilt sank in. If only he'd just left her alone to ski as she pleased, she probably wouldn't be in this mess and in pain. He skied as fast as he could, knowing he needed to be more cautious because it wouldn't help Aubrey if he injured himself on the way down.

Once he made it to the lodge and spoke to the rescue team, they suited up within minutes, slinging backpacks over their shoulders. Gabe followed them out to the lift, his heart pounding the entire time. The two rescuers got on the lift just before him, and he just hoped that Aubrey would be okay when they found her.

What if she'd gone unconscious? He replayed everything in his mind from the time he stopped and turned around, but he couldn't remember if she'd hit her head or not. His heartbeat echoed in his ears, making him wish he could somehow speed up the lift.

Once they made it to the top, Gabe skied down after the guy and girl, yelling out to direct them how far down. They slowed down with relative ease after going so fast, and Gabe was grateful to see their skill as they approached her.

"Where is the injury?" the woman asked, kneeling in the snow.

Aubrey glanced up at Gabe with a pained smile before turning her attention to the woman. "My knee popped, and with all the symptoms I'm feeling, it's quite likely that I tore my ACL, MCL, or both."

The woman did a few checks around the knee and leg, nodding a bit when Aubrey mentioned if it hurt or not. "I think your assessment is correct, miss. Doctor?"

"Nurse. I've treated this dozens of times. I didn't expect I'd be going through the same thing, though." The group chuckled at Aubrey's comments, and Gabe was amazed by her ability to stay calm and joke, even when he could see her gritting her teeth in pain.

The male rescuer worked to pump up an inflatable sled with a manual pump, and Gabe thought it would take quite a while to get it ready. But after watching Aubrey for several more seconds, he saw the sled was ready for her. Gabe helped move her over to the bright orange sled and held onto her hand for a moment as the rescuers readied for the descent.

Rushing to put his skis back on, Gabe caught up with them, skiing alongside Aubrey. She had her eyes closed, and a single tear slipped out, sliding down the side of her face. The scene triggered a memory in his brain, something he'd no doubt pushed as far back as possible. Nicoletta had done something similar, twisting her leg halfway down the mountain once when they'd come skiing together. And she'd done it after he'd challenged her to a race down the mountain.

Would he ever learn? The guilt plowed into his stomach like a boulder, and he looked up to focus on the rest of the descent to the lodge. He was falling for this girl, but how would she ever be able to trust him after he'd jeopardized her health?

CHAPTER 21

"Can I get you anything?" Gabe asked, staring down at her on the couch. The deep line in his forehead hadn't budged since they'd made it back to the hotel. He'd insisted on carrying her to the room and had worked so hard to make sure she was comfortable.

"Some ice to start. Do they have some ibuprofen or pain pills down in the lobby? I'm just glad the medical team had a compression wrap. That will help for when I need to get up."

Gabe moved forward, looking as though he was going to pick her up. "Well, I can help you with anything you need."

Aubrey shook her head. "I'd prefer to get to the bathroom by myself, but thank you." She watched as his cheeks changed to a bright pink.

After a small shift so her legs were elevated with a pillow underneath, she closed her eyes, exhausted from the craziness of the day. As much as it would be nice to be home so her mother could dote on her for a few days, she much preferred seeing a doctor who Gabe trusted to get the final results.

When the rescue woman had agreed that it was probably a

torn ACL, Aubrey was somewhat relieved to have a second opinion. She'd been in a lot of pain and wasn't sure if that might have clouded her diagnosis. Once they got back to Marghera, she'd see a doctor and then change her flight to head home. It was always better to travel with a doctor's note to get the extra accommodations she would need with her knee like it was.

She slipped into a light sleep, waking only to take some pain pills and adjust the ice when Gabe brought it to her. There wasn't much to do, so she told Gabe to go back to his room, promising to call if she needed anything more.

"Are you hungry? Can I get you any food?" From the worry in his voice, she wondered if he was trying to atone for something.

"Maybe just a sandwich and some fruit or chips? Whatever you can get here." That would have been what she'd want in the States, but did they have that kind of stuff in hotels in Italy?

Gabe nodded, his lips pressed into a thin line. "Okay, I'll go find something for you. Rest up." He leaned down and pressed a kiss to her forehead, causing her to smile.

"You're amazing. You know that, right?" she said, her eyes heavily lidded. She didn't see his face but heard faint footsteps.

Once the click of the door sounded, Aubrey didn't remember much, the exhaustion taking over. When she woke, she saw it was almost nine, and it took a minute to realize that it was lighter outside, meaning she'd survived the night.

Sitting up a bit, everything was wet around her knee, and the bag that had once held the ice was completely empty. A knock sounded on the door, and she called out, "Come in."

Gabe walked in, his hair ruffled and dark circles under his eyes, looking like he hadn't slept at all the night before.

There was a chair next to the couch with a rumpled blanket where he must have sat with her through the night, and Aubrey had been covered with one as well.

"Sorry I slept so long. I just woke up." She yawned, trying to cover it with her hand.

With a shake of his head, Gabe said, "Don't worry. I just woke up a few minutes ago. I figured I'd let you sleep as long as possible this morning. I'm sure your body is trying to recover."

He removed the bag of water and retrieved a towel from the bathroom, mopping up the wet mess around her leg. He then placed a fresh bag of ice on her knee. With a glass of orange juice, he handed her two pain pills. "Take these so you don't feel the pain."

Taking them from his palm, she smirked before she tossed them into her mouth. "Look who's the nurse now."

He gave her a weak smile, and she had a niggling feeling that something was off this morning.

As Aubrey raised her hands over her head, she could feel the stiffness in her ribs and side that hit the ground when she landed. Her wrist had some pain, but it was nothing more than a sprained muscle, meaning she just needed to focus on her knee at the moment.

"Do we need to pack up and get going?" she asked, adjusting the ice.

Gabe took a seat on the bed, his face crestfallen like he had to deliver the worst news in the world. "There was a big storm last night. All the roads in and out of here are blocked off at least until tomorrow or Tuesday."

Aubrey sank back into her pillows. Not that she had much of a choice now as touring different European cities would be hard on crutches.

"Okay. So we're stuck inside for a couple of days. Do they

have any movies we could borrow? I don't know if I can lie on this couch that long without going stir-crazy."

Gabe stood and moved to stand by the couch. "What can I get to make you more comfortable?"

"I've got ice for now, but thank you. I have a tablet in my bag over there. I can get caught up on some of the reading I've been putting off." She gave him a small smile, trying to ease the anxiety she saw on his face. What was going on inside him that he could look so tortured and wounded?

"Are you all right?" Aubrey asked, trying to get him to look at her. "You look like you're going to have a breakdown or something."

"Yeah, I'm fine. Just a long night, and I feel bad you're hurting." He grimaced as if seeing the scene before his eyes once more.

Aubrey grinned. "It's fine. I'll be fine. We can't do much to change it now, so let's just roll with it."

"Let me see about some movies, and we'll figure out what to do for the rest of the time." He retrieved her tablet for her and nodded his head before disappearing out the door.

The silence in the room made Aubrey cringe, feeling guilt that she had traveled thousands of miles to visit Europe, and now she was incapacitated and unable to leave because of the weather.

Once the ice had been on for long enough, she stood and hopped on her good leg to the bed. From there, she made it to the wall and then to her luggage. After a long day of skiing, she could use a good hot shower. Pulling out her clothes, she hobbled into the bathroom and locked it, not wanting Gabe to accidentally walk in.

She spent much longer in the shower than she normally did, but maneuvering was a problem. After throwing on her clothes, she moved back into the room, hopping along like a bunny to avoid using her injured leg. She grabbed her brush and moved it through her long hair, jumping when she saw something out of the corner of her eye.

Gabe stuck his hands out and said, "It's just me. Sorry. Are you all right?" He walked up to her, his eyes moving over her body as if checking for additional injuries.

"I'm fine, Gabe." She leaned in and gave him a hug, holding on tight and letting some of the stress she'd felt over getting hurt in a foreign country seep out of her. "You've taken care of me so well, and for that, I'm so grateful."

"Can I help you over to the couch again? I found some food and refilled another bag of ice." The corner of his mouth turned up, and Aubrey reached up and kissed him quickly.

She was grateful when he picked her up and set her back on the couch. Her left leg hurt enough from hopping around the room that she didn't know if she'd make it back to her original spot on her own.

She glanced at the phone next to her on the coffee table. Should she call her mother and tell her what was going on? They'd talked only a few days before, but it had been brief because the cost of it was going to skyrocket her monthly phone bill.

She reached over and took the phone, entering the code to unlock the screen. Instead of dialing the number she'd memorized when her mother finally got a cell phone during Aubrey's fifth-grade year, she clicked on the gallery icon, opening all the pictures she'd taken over her time in Europe.

There were so many beautiful landscapes and venues she'd seen, but her favorite so far was the selfie she'd taken in the tower with Gabe. It had been the perfect morning, something she wasn't sure could ever be topped. She just wished she knew what was really going on and not the fake answer he'd given her earlier. It would be a challenge to date long-distance, but she wanted to at least try if he was interested.

"What were you able to scrounge up?" she asked, turning to look at Gabe in the chair next to her. His mouth had softened at the edges since he'd gone down to the office, and Aubrey hoped that was a good sign.

"We're in luck. They only had a few—how do you call them in America? 'Chick-flicks'? But they're in Italian, so I hope you're ready to learn." He smiled, pushing a DVD into the player Aubrey hadn't seen as it was hidden in the drawers.

"I do know Spanish. Italian shouldn't be that hard to learn, right?" She winked at him, taking a small bag of something chocolate from his outstretched hand and opening it up to eat.

"I'm impressed. Most of the Americans I met at Hawthorne thought it was a waste of time to learn another language."

Aubrey chuckled a bit, knowing the type of student to say that, usually the ones who were failing or struggling to understand the language. "It's definitely been handy, especially when I worked in the emergency room. It was hard to communicate with some people, but when they would find out that I'd learned their language, they were grateful they could at least understand what I was explaining to them as far as what would come next in the process of their stay."

"Let me move you to the bed. Your back could probably use a change from the couch." Gabe moved before she could even say anything, resting her on the untouched pillows from the night before.

The opening credits began, and Aubrey was surprised when Gabe sat next to her on the bed, his back propped up against the wall. He'd brought several other treats Aubrey had never seen or heard of, but as she tried each one, she realized how good they were. Except for the anise-flavored one. She had to spit it out on a tissue Gabe retrieved for her.

"You don't like that kind, huh?"

Aubrey snuck another hazelnut and shook her head. "Not so much. I didn't know if it would taste better here, but I'm not a fan."

They spent the rest of the afternoon watching romantic comedies, and with the subtitles on, Aubrey was picking up more and more Italian. She moved her hand to take his and tried to hide the smile as his thumb rubbed the back of her hand. Glancing over at him for a moment here and there, her thoughts wandered to whether learning Italian would be worthwhile in her future. She'd studied Spanish at the behest of her mother who'd said she could always use it, especially as a nurse. But Italian wouldn't be as common, especially when she went back to the States once she was able to travel.

She fell asleep at one point and opened her eyes to see her head was resting on Gabe's stomach. With the even and deep breathing coming from him, she knew he was asleep as well, which helped her go back to sleep.

By the time she woke up, she could tell she'd slept longer than she should have because of the struggle it was to wake up and the ache in her knee. At least the ice had kept some of the swelling down. She turned to find Gabe was gone, and she felt his absence.

Opening up a new text message, she typed in, *Where did you go?*

She stared at the screen until it darkened, wondering if he'd respond quickly. He probably had enough to worry about without her constantly bugging him for things.

After flipping through channels on the regular television twice, Aubrey turned it off and pulled out her tablet to read one of the books she'd begun on the plane ten days ago. The plot pulled her in even more now, as the scenario seemed oddly familiar to her situation.

The door opened, and Gabe walked in, looking as if he'd been awake for days, his hair standing on end.

"What happened to you?" Aubrey asked, putting her tablet on the bed next to her. "Where did you go?"

Gabe raked a hand through his hair, making even more of it stick out all over. "Just a lot going on all at once. I went to check on the road conditions and get you some, drum roll, ice!" The look on his face was the most relaxed she'd seen him since she'd fallen on the mountain.

Aubrey patted the bed, and when he sat down, she pulled him so his head was resting on her lap. She moved her hands through his soft short hair, much like her mother had done to Aubrey when she was stressed as a teen.

"I'm here if you need to talk about anything. I'm sorry I pulled you away from work and then got us stuck up here."

Gabe didn't move, and for a second, Aubrey wondered if he'd already fallen asleep. He finally said, "It's not your fault, and it's been a lot of fun. More fun than I've had in a while."

"I seem to remember you mucking out stalls at my family's ranch. Are you sure this has been more fun than that?" She poked at his side, and he jumped, moving to guard that area. Aubrey moved to poke another part of his back, and he sat up, a wide grin on his face.

"Yes, definitely more fun than that." He began another movie and scooted back to sit next to her against the headboard, and Aubrey slipped her hand next to his, intertwining their fingers. He didn't react to it much, but Aubrey's heart skipped a beat as she thought about this guy sitting next to her.

The smell of his cologne and the electricity flowing between their hands brought a sadness to her when she thought about leaving Italy in a few days. That was her luck, though.

CHAPTER 22

Gabe did his best not to stiffen when Aubrey took his hand. The guilt over her injury ate at him. If he hadn't been so stubborn or pushy, she wouldn't be in pain. The softness of her skin against his palm eased some of the anxiety brewing in his gut, but he still didn't feel like he was worthy of the beautiful girl sitting next to him.

On top of the guilt over Aubrey's accident, the memories of Nicoletta's ski accident wouldn't leave him either. Gabe had taken off down one of the steeper slopes to beat her. When he'd made it down the hill, she didn't come for several minutes, and then a couple came skiing slowly with her in between them. He remembered the guilt filling him as a teenager, that he hadn't been the one to help her down the mountain and had just worried about himself. After her death, Nicoletta's parents had told him that it was actually something that helped them find the cancer with all the scans she'd had to have, giving her several extra months with the treatments.

And now, here he was in a similar situation, with Aubrey

injured. Would the same thing happen? Would she leave and have some illness and never tell him about it?

Gabe shook his head, concentrating on the screen in front of him. A movie played that looked somewhat familiar, but it wasn't registering.

Who was he kidding? She would leave Italy and never look back, never worry about him again. But part of him didn't feel that was completely correct, that Aubrey wasn't that type of woman. He just needed to get out of this hotel room and back to Venice. Maybe things would figure themselves out there.

IT HAD TAKEN SOME DOING, but they were able to get Aubrey situated somewhat comfortably in Gabe's car on Monday around mid-morning. He hoped they'd be able to avoid the big traffic, but he was grateful to be out of the hotel room and going back to some kind of schedule, something he didn't usually fail at or hurt anyone doing. It had been nice to relax and watch movies, as well as talk with Aubrey about different subjects, but she was missing the rest of her European trip because he'd been stupid.

Aubrey leaned forward and pressed buttons for the radio, settling on a soft classical song. She leaned her head back and closed her eyes, making her look angelic and even more beautiful. There was no way he had a chance of a future with her. Ever since the accident, he'd felt like a bumbling idiot, stiff and not himself. He told himself that if he just hoped enough, Aubrey's scans would be clean when they made it to a doctor in a few hours.

The skies were still gray, but the roads were clear, the wall of snow from the plows reaching a height higher than his car.

It felt a lot like they were driving through a white tunnel, and Gabe made sure to keep his eyes on the narrow two-lane road, hoping to avoid any further accidents and injuries.

"How are you feeling? Do you need any medicine for the pain?" Gabe asked, adjusting the temperature higher. His windshield was fogging up quickly, and he needed the heat focused on it to see the road properly.

"I'm good," Aubrey said, opening her lids only a slit. She smiled at him and closed them again. She'd slept quite a bit the past day, but after all the traveling and the injury, he could imagine it was good for her.

They made the drive in adequate time, stopping off outside a large building several blocks from his parents' home.

Aubrey opened her eyes, blinking several times, and Gabe grinned, loving the way she tried to wake up. "Where are we?" she asked.

"Here to see a doctor."

She frowned. "You already have an appointment?"

With a half-smile, he said, "My mom made one for you. I think she kind of likes you."

"I like her. She's like my own mother in so many ways. It will be hard to say goodbye when I have to go home." Aubrey's smile fell, and she looked down at her hands. From her words, a small flame of hope flared to life inside Gabe's chest.

He turned toward her, resting his one hand on the steering wheel and his other elbow on the back of the seat. "Do you think you'll stay in California forever?" He blinked a few times, surprised that the words had actually escaped his lips.

Aubrey moved her gaze to his. "I'm not sure. Before I came to Europe, I was thinking of finding a job closer to the ranch. But now that I've been here, I don't know. The possibilities are limitless."

Gabe opened his mouth to ask another question, hesitated, and then his mind went blank. He smiled at her and said, "We should probably get inside. Wait there, and I'll come help you."

After several minutes of maneuvering, they made it through the doors of the private clinic his mother had taken him and Sophia to for years when they were growing up. He helped Aubrey rest in a chair and went to the counter to check them in.

It took much longer than he was used to as Aubrey was an American and processing the correct paperwork took time. He handed a credit card to the woman behind the desk and told her to put the cost of the consultation on it, knowing Aubrey wasn't part of the healthcare system there.

When he sat down next to her, she leaned her head on his shoulder. "Thanks for doing that. How much do I need to pay you?"

Gabe shook his head, inhaling the vanilla scent of her shampoo as he did and relaxing against the back of the chair. "Nothing. I was the one who caused you to be in this mess."

Aubrey jerked back to frown at him. "None of this was your fault. Is that why you've been so weird this weekend? You can't blame yourself that I barely hit a rock, tumbled, and tore some ligaments."

Grabbing her hand, Gabe tried to smile, but the attempt wasn't successful. "When you say it like that, I really feel horrible. I was the one who challenged you to a race."

Aubrey's name was called before she could respond, and she flashed him a glare that said, *This isn't over.*

The doctor did several movement tests and then had the nurse take Aubrey back for an MRI, the results showing a torn ACL. Gabe's stomach sank as he realized what it would take for her to recover. Surgery, weeks of therapy, and probably not back to normal for another six months. That's what had happened to Nicoletta, and it seemed like she'd had to go to physical therapy so often that he barely saw her before he left for Hawthorne his freshman year.

His eyes clouded as they waited for the nurse to bring in a brace for her knee, and Aubrey must have seen it.

"Come here," she said from the examination table.

Gabe stood from his chair and took a few steps forward, looking down at her.

Aubrey moved to a sitting position and took her thumb, wiping underneath his eyes. "It's okay. It's not your fault. This might have happened on another part of my trip, and who would I have been able to depend on then?" She grinned and wrapped her arms around him, pulling him close.

The hug eased his worries again, but only somewhat. He knew she was trying to make him feel better, but the guilt had already dug in deep enough to allow the roots to grow.

"I, uh, Nicoletta was hurt one time when we went skiing, and I found out later that they found the cancer because of the scans." Everything came out in a harsh whisper as a few tears slid down his cheeks and onto her hair.

Aubrey looked up. "Why didn't you tell me? There was no cancer on any of the scans the doctor just took. I'm a healthy twenty-nine-year-old, other than the fact I have to hobble like I'm ninety at the moment." She grinned at him and pulled his chin up so their eyes met.

"That's a relief," Gabe said, feeling only a small part of his anxiety dissipate. "Have you talked to your family?"

She pulled back, giving him a sheepish expression. "No, I haven't really talked to them since I saw you near the piazza."

"You might want to give them a call. Your mother can arrange the surgery and everything." He handed her his phone. "Use this. I've got it set for international calls."

She took it gratefully and dialed her mother's phone number. When she put the phone to her ear, a knock came at the door, and the doctor walked in for a moment.

"She'll need a bit of rest, but the swelling has started to go down already, probably due to her skills as a nurse and knowing what to do. I'd recommend surgery as soon as possible to allow her to get back to work. She probably won't be able to do more than desk work, if that, until she's fully healed."

Gabe nodded, taking the final paperwork. Not only had he spoiled her European vacation, but he'd caused her to miss work for the next six months. As much as he felt the responsibility to the people of Marghera and his family and workers, this weighed on him even more.

Aubrey hung up the phone a few minutes later and handed it back to him. She took the pair of crutches they'd brought in for her and moved off the table. "Did they say we can go?"

"Yes. How was talking to your mom?" Gabe asked, holding the door open for her.

"She wasn't too surprised. She's been through a lot of injuries with my brothers. My older brother, Darren, tore his ACL and MCL when he was playing football in high school. It took a long time for him to heal, the baby." She chuckled, and Gabe followed, needing something to assuage the pit in his chest and stomach.

As they neared the car, Gabe moved to open the door for her and was surprised when she leaned the crutches against the side of the car and pulled him to her. Their lips met, and it was the same fiery sensation as on the mountain. She'd told him several times it wasn't his fault, and he was starting to believe it. Now the biggest obstacle was how to date this amazing woman when she was an ocean away.

CHAPTER 23

*A*ubrey woke up later than she'd planned the next morning, hoping she hadn't inconvenienced anyone's plans by sleeping so late. She pulled on a pair of sweats and a sweater before hobbling out into the family room. No one was in the kitchen, but she didn't want to go poking around the house to see if anyone was still home.

Walking over to the fridge, she found a note in cursive. It took some time to figure out what it said, as she hadn't seen writing like this since her grandmother passed away fifteen years before.

Breakfast is in the oven. I'll be back in a few hours.

Aubrey opened the oven to find what she would call an American breakfast of bacon, eggs, and toast. Opening the fridge door, she found some juice, which Amara had somehow discovered was a favorite. She took a seat at the table and took small bites of the semi-warm food.

Pulling out her phone, she checked to see if she had any messages, a small part of her hoping Gabe had wished her a good morning or at least asked how she was doing. Her screen lit up with a picture of her older brother, Darren's two kids, but there was no message from Gabe. She swiped to check some of the apps she hadn't looked at in almost two weeks.

It didn't take long to get bored of those, and she finished the food, feeling much better than she had for a few days. She and Gabe hadn't really talked about what was going to happen or when she would be officially leaving, but something made Aubrey want to hang on a couple of days.

She laughed softly. What was she expecting? That the gorgeous Italian man who had the fate of a lot of people's livelihoods in his hands would just magically go down on one knee and ask her to stay forever? As much as she tried to shake it off, that fantasy was more hope than she'd had in a long time.

Deciding she didn't need to wait for him to contact her, she opened a new text to him and tapped away at the keyboard.

I hope you slept well and you don't have too much to catch up on. Let me know what your plans are for this evening.

She could feel her heartbeat in her throat as she read and reread the words. Finally deciding it was good enough, she pressed send and clicked her screen off. The temptation to stare at the screen until a response appeared was tempting, but she knew she needed to decide what to do. Did she stick around, waiting for the Gabe from the tower and the first part of the skiing trip to come back? Or did she just hope he would get out of whatever funk he was in and go back to the talkative and fun Gabe he'd been as her tour guide?

She knew it was going to inflate her phone bill through the roof, but she needed to talk to someone, and that someone was Sadie. She'd always had sound advice for Aubrey before. This was one of those times where Aubrey was stuck, not knowing which direction to turn.

The phone rang several times before a groggy voice answered, "Hello?"

Aubrey froze, checking the time on the clock on the wall. It was nearly ten in the morning here, meaning that it was four o'clock in New York where Sadie was working.

"Oh my goodness! Sadie, I didn't realize it was so early there. I'll call you later so you can go back to sleep."

A groan echoed through the line, and Sadie said, "No, I'm up. I've been wondering how your trip has been going, but I didn't want to bug you too much."

Aubrey smiled. Sadie was a true friend, and she didn't know if she could ever repay her for all she'd done to help Aubrey in all the situations she'd gotten herself into.

"It's been going pretty well, except I tore my ACL skiing the other day."

"What? Your mom didn't tell us that. She just said you were hanging out with Gabe and his family for a few days."

With a sigh, Aubrey said, "Of course, she'd choose to omit the painful part."

"Well? How are things going? I'm kind of surprised you've been willingly hanging out with Gabe. Evan said sparks were flying between you two at the retreat, but not the good kind."

Laughing out loud, Aubrey nodded her head in the empty room. "Well, that's probably true. But when I got to know him here in his element, he's actually a lot different than I labeled him at the ranch."

"Different as in what?" Aubrey could hear the smile in Sadie's voice, and part of her just wanted to gush, but the hot and cold signals from Gabe the past two days put a stop to that.

"He's a good guy. A little more involved in work than I would like, but I, well, I kind of like him. I just don't know how he feels about me. There were several moments where I thought he really liked me too, but ever since I tore my ACL, it's like he's struggling to be around me. I think he blames himself that it happened at all."

Aubrey took a breath, hoping Sadie would break in with some great analysis. When the silence continued, she said, "He asked me if I was planning to live in California the rest of my life but then stopped the conversation after I said probably not. I'm just so confused right now. Are Italian men supposed to be as frustrating as American ones?"

Sadie laughed out loud and then softened it. "Just a minute, and I'll move to the next room. Evan's still sleeping, and I don't want to wake him." Aubrey heard her take several breaths and then a soft click of a door several thousand miles away. "You know what you have to do, right?"

"What?" Aubrey groaned, knowing whatever Sadie was about to suggest was going to be more painful than she wanted it to be.

"You'll need to talk to him. Tell him how you feel, and then see what he says. If he says he doesn't think of you like that, then at least you put yourself out there and you can come home without regrets. If he says he feels the same, figure out a way to make it work between you two. Communication, Aubrey. There's a lot that can be solved with a few bits of courage and talking."

Tilting her head back so it leaned on the chair, Aubrey closed her eyes a few moments, feeling like a hurricane was moving through her stomach, the anxiety twisting and turning.

"You're probably right, Sadie. I should let you get to bed so you're not exhausted when it's a normal time to get up. Tell Evan hi for me."

"Will do. Good luck, Aubs. You can do it!"

The line clicked, and Aubrey set the phone down on the table in front of her. How was she going to make it through a conversation like that? She'd had a hard enough time breaking up with Lance several months before, and she almost backed out halfway through when he started tearing up. The jerk had cheated on her and made her feel guilty for breaking up.

A text sounded, and she turned the phone back over. Gabe's name popped onto her screen, and she opened it quickly, hoping it would be some sign of his feelings.

Thanks. Sorry I didn't get a chance to stop by this morning. I'm just trying to catch up. I should be done for a late dinner. Are you up for that?

Aubrey responded with an affirmative answer faster than she thought possible, and she just hoped she'd feel this optimistic by tonight.

CHAPTER 24

Gabe had made it into the office early that morning, knowing how much he'd already missed since Aubrey had arrived. Sophia had done an okay job considering the limited amount of training he'd given her, but there was still a lot of undone paperwork and several meetings to prepare for that day.

When a text message sounded around ten, he smiled when he saw Aubrey's name and her text. He felt pulled toward her, but there was also something restraining him, like he was at a standstill, unable to move forward or back. She'd said it wasn't his fault that she'd gotten hurt. He'd accepted that fact. But even with the scans clean of cancer, how did he know she wouldn't tire of him and go back home to America at the first chance?

The fact that she hadn't contacted her family since he'd seen her on the dock was a big deal, as he knew how close she was with her mother and family. But that could only last so long before she was homesick. If they were to pursue a relationship, would he always feel the guilt of taking her away from her family? Because while they could visit for holidays, there was no way he could leave Italy to live in the States, due to the company.

So many questions for a girl he'd spent less than a week with total, but he knew that if he let them, his feelings for her would overtake any rational part of his mind that he left unguarded.

After Aubrey said she'd be up for a late dinner, he sent another message. *I'll pick you up around eight. I'll make sure we don't have to walk too far.*

His phone rang after he hit send. Max was trying to video call.

Answering, Gabe said, "Do you not work ever?"

"What are you talking about? I'm checking on one of my stores right now. Well, leaving it, actually. I haven't heard from you in a while and thought I'd check in. I know how you get when you lose yourself in work." Max held the phone so close to his face that all Gabe could see was the smattering of freckles across his nose, his breathing signaling he was walking somewhere.

"It hasn't all been work the past few days. Aubrey Pearson showed up in Venice last Thursday."

"What?" Max pulled the phone back farther to get a good look at Gabe. "Have you been hanging out with her?"

"Yeah. She's different than I expected, and she's a lot of fun. Except for the fact that I caused her to tear her ACL." Gabe looked away, not wanting to meet Max's stare.

When Max didn't say anything, Gabe turned back to the screen. "Come on, man. You didn't cause her to tear it, just like you didn't cause Nicoletta's cancer. If you've got feelings for her, go for it."

"Go for what? A long-distance relationship where we see each other twice a year for three years before we decide it's too hard and then break up?"

Max gave him a casual shrug of the shoulders. "Have you talked to her about it? That could be a place to start."

"We're both close to our families. How much more guilt would I have to feel from tearing her away from her family?" A mound formed in his throat. He hadn't consciously thought of it that way before, but he knew it was true. He knew he liked Aubrey enough to want to pursue a relationship, but was it fair to make her give up her family for him and to live minutes from his?

"Hey, remember me? Single friend? I don't know how that plays out, but if you feel like you should pursue it, maybe you should."

Gabe smiled, trying to move the mass in his throat and not succeeding. "What's going on with you? Any women catch your eye yet?"

"No, but make sure your mom doesn't give mine any pointers anymore. My mom tried to set me up on a date last weekend. I'm not ready for that kind of pressure."

That got Gabe laughing harder than he had in days. "Well, you should have never caved and given your mom the number for mine. At least you understand how I feel to some degree."

"I need to get to another appointment because I do, in fact, work. But when you get a chance, come to Munich for the weekend. We can have fun and take your mind off things if you need to."

Gabe nodded. "Thanks, Max. I'll have to do that when I get caught up on life here. Good luck with your appointment."

They hung up, and Gabe had a good feeling. He still had no idea what he was going to do or say when he saw Aubrey, but for the first time in two days, he hoped she'd want to pursue a relationship too.

ubrey had spent the day hobbling around a few of the nearby streets, needing to get outside of the walls of a building for longer than a few minutes. She was surprised at how stir-crazy she was becoming, but this was the first major injury she'd ever had, besides breaking her hand in a softball game when she was ten. She'd never been so restricted, and she could feel the ache in her underarms from the crutches.

Amara had made sure she sat down the minute she walked in the door, bringing her ice and some painkillers, and although Aubrey wanted to say she didn't need either, her body told a different story.

When it neared eight o'clock, Aubrey made sure to change into a fresh shirt and ran a brush through her hair, not having the energy to curl her long locks.

Eight thirty came and went, then nine. She didn't so much as receive a message. Amara had given her a small portion of what she'd made for dinner, knowing Gabe was supposed to be there much sooner. She'd apologized several times about Gabe's tardiness, reminding Aubrey of her mother. The madder she got about Gabe being late, the more she just wanted to be in the safety of her parents' home where she wouldn't have to worry about being stood up while staying in the guy's parents' home.

Finally, closer to ten, Aubrey said goodnight to the Alessandros, using her crutches to make it down the short hall to the room she was staying in. She changed into her pajamas without so much as a flicker of emotion, but as she sank into the bed, pulling the covers over her shoulders, she sobbed quietly.

This wouldn't be as easy to get over as all her other relationships. She'd fallen for Gabriele Alessandro, and it looked as though things were one-sided.

* * *

SHE AWOKE a couple hours later with the urgent need to find a bathroom. As she walked out of the room, she heard hushed voices and wondered who in the family would stay up this late.

Edging her way against the wall since she'd forgotten her crutches in the sleep-induced haze, she peeked around the corner to see the back of Gabe and his father sitting on the couch. They often spoke in English when she was around, Gabe's father's knowledge of her native language near the same level as Gabe's. But why they would be speaking English with her not in the room, she wasn't sure.

"You really need to get an alarm or something, mio figlio. You're working yourself to an early grave if you don't take some time off to sleep and eat."

"I know, Dad. I didn't know it was almost midnight until I looked at the clock." He ran a hand through his hair, blowing out an audible breath. "I feel awful about Aubrey. Was she okay that I didn't make it?"

Giovanni shrugged. "I'm not sure. She waited out here until nearly ten, and she looked disappointed when she went to bed. What are you doing? Do you have feelings for her?"

"I do. There are times when I think we could make it work, that to have her by my side would help me push back from work a bit more, delegate the tasks I don't need to do."

"Just like tonight?" Giovanni asked, his tone sounding unsure.

Aubrey had to duck back against the wall for a moment. She hadn't had a good chance to get to know Gabe's dad very well, but she did like his honesty and bluntness.

"I just don't know what to do, Dad. Is it fair to ask her to give up her life in America? What if she stays here a few months and decides this isn't what she wants? How do I go on from there?"

"Well, is it fair to promise her a night out when she's been stuck here all day and then not show up? First things first, she needs to get home and have surgery. You can figure out all the details from there. But for once, put yourself above the business. You deserve it, Gabe. You've worked hard over the past few years, and I know you don't want to lose ground, but if all you have to show for your life is work, you're going to be pretty miserable later on."

Gabe nodded. "I'll fly her home. She'll be more comfortable in my plane than in a commercial one."

"What about Bianchi? I heard he wanted you to come to some big event for Nicoletta."

"What was I supposed to say, Dad? We're donors for the charity he runs in Nicoletta's name. She was a great part of my past—"

From the tone in his voice, Aubrey turned away, feeling the sadness sink into her stomach. She couldn't bear to hear more. Was he really over his ex-girlfriend? As much as she liked hearing about Gabe's feelings for Aubrey, she deserved someone who could give their whole heart, not just a few leftover bits of it.

She shuffled back to bed, knowing sleep wasn't going to come easy now.

CHAPTER 26

Gabe woke up with a stiff neck the next morning. He'd decided to crash at his parents' house, and since Aubrey was staying in his old room, he'd slept on the couch. Opening up his phone, he made a note to get his parents a new couch, knowing that after more than thirty years, they deserved a new one, and so did their guests.

He was grateful for the conversation he'd had with his father. He'd attend the event for Nicoletta's charity and then fly Aubrey home. Most of all, he knew she was what he wanted in his future. He just felt bad that he'd stayed so late at the office, looking through the dozens of applications he'd already received on the three positions he'd listed on a few credible websites. He could feel that sliver of freedom he'd had in Utah growing, and days off with Aubrey wouldn't be a huge burden on just one person covering for him.

He walked into the kitchen, the light from the sun just barely peeking through the windows.

"What are you doing up, Gabe? You got in late and then talked to your father well into the night." His mother cut several slices of bread and placed them in a basket, along with several jams and butter. She moved around the counter and set it on the table just as Sophia walked in.

"What happened to you? You look like you've aged at least ten years in the last few days." Sophia touched his face and flicked his cheek with her finger, causing Gabe to flinch back. As the irritation spread over his cheek, he lunged in her direction, hoping to inflict the same pain.

Their mother stood between them, her small stature not too intimidating but the look on her face causing them to back down. "Sit. Eat. You both have a lot to do today."

Footsteps came from the hall, and Aubrey stood in the doorway, looking how Gabe felt. He smiled up at her, but she avoided his gaze. He probably deserved that.

"How did you sleep?" he asked, standing to pull out a chair for her.

"Fine, thank you." Her voice was soft but clipped, and as much as he didn't want an audience when he apologized to her, he didn't know if she'd hear him out if he waited any longer.

He reached over, covering her hand with his. "I'm really sorry about last night. I don't have an excuse other than not checking the time."

"Don't worry about it." Aubrey flicked her hair back over her shoulder and leaned over to retrieve a slice of bread from the basket.

His heart sank. This wasn't going to be as easy as he'd hoped. "My dad and I were talking last night, and I think it would be best if I fly you home in my jet. You'll have plenty of room for your leg and won't have any layovers. Do you mind if we leave on Thursday? I have a few meetings between now and then, but Sophia can take over the business for a few days while I'm gone."

Aubrey looked him in the eyes for the first time since entering the room and paused as if searching for something.

"Yeah, I think that would work." She turned her attention back to the slice of bread in her hand, working to spread butter to every inch of the crust.

Gabe took a slice of his own and added marmalade to it, standing after he put the knife back. "I've got to head home and change, but I'll see you all later." He turned to Aubrey. "Can we reschedule our dinner for tonight?" His heart thundered in his chest. He knew she was mad, but he hoped he could make it up to her.

"Sure," Aubrey said, not looking up.

Well, at least he had some hope. He just hoped she wasn't like this at dinner.

* * *

AUBREY BREATHED a sigh of relief when Gabe left. She wished that his touch didn't cause her stomach to flip and her pulse to race, because it would make what she had to do that much easier.

Sophia left the house with Gabe, and Amara had some luncheon she had to attend, even though she'd offered to skip it several times. Aubrey had refused her every time.

It was time to go home. After a twenty-minute phone call to the airlines, she was able to upgrade her seat to business class, which nearly emptied her bank account after the exploits of the past two weeks.

Bag packed and a car called, she made her way to the airport, silently saying goodbye to the empty home. If Gabe was still conflicted about a relationship over a decade old and with work as busy as it was, she was better to leave now. More to guard her heart than anything.

CHAPTER 27

"What do you want, Aiden?" Aubrey was surprised by the bite in her voice, but she'd had a long trip with all of her stops on the way home to the ranch. She was just grateful to be on the ground for more than a few hours again.

"Just thought I'd call to see how my baby sister is," he said, a smile in his voice.

"Oh please, we're almost thirty. I was born a whole minute after you, so don't go starting with that stuff. Why are you calling Mom's phone to talk to me?" She shifted, wishing she had already had the surgery and could begin to recover. Her mother had worked a miracle and got her a time for the next day, which would help her focus on the pain of her recovery rather than her broken heart.

Aiden sighed. "Because yours is turned off. What happened, Aubs? Gabe has been calling every few hours since this morning, California time."

"Honestly, I have no idea. I started to have feelings for him," she paused a moment, feeling weird about telling one of her triplet brothers about a crush she had on one of his good friends. Well, more than a crush, because the dull ache from being single felt like it had been ripped right open. "But since I hurt my leg, he acted all weird, withdrawn. He's got a lot going on with work, and I knew I'd never be a priority in his life, not like Mom is with Dad." Not to mention his heart was still partly taken.

She felt hot tears forming, and she wiped them away, not wanting to cry over a dumb guy.

"How do you know you wouldn't be a priority? Maybe he just needs to make a few changes to get to that point." Aiden's voice was smooth and relaxed, just as it always was. Not judging, only pointing out life tips that usually helped her when she stopped being stubborn enough to see it.

Shaking her head, she looked up at the ceiling, not sure what to say. "I left a note thanking his family for their kindness. I was just ready to go home, get the surgery, get through therapy. Move on with my life. Remember Italy as a dream." She bit her lip, trying to keep the emotion from her voice.

"Well, don't give up completely. There is a perfect guy for you who will come along. It might still be Gabe, if you let him."

Wiping her nose with a tissue, Aubrey said, "Time will tell, I guess. What about you? You need to find yourself a girl."

"Not many girls like to date a shy billionaire that dreads going to parties and events. But life is good. I'm not complaining." His comment made Aubrey smile. How was it that her triplet brothers looked identical but their personalities were so different from one another? But the three of them balanced each other out, so it worked in the end.

"I'm going to rest up. Surgery is tomorrow, so say a little prayer that I come out alive."

"Better you than me. I think I'd pass out if I had to have

surgery right now. Good luck, sis. I'll come to the ranch when I can."

When they hung up, Aubrey stared at the large glass windows looking out into the backyard of the farmhouse her parents had lived in for as long as she could remember. If Gabe were to show up at the door right then, what would she say or do? Her feelings of pain and love tumbled together inside her, making it difficult for her to know what she would say.

She knew that a life with Gabriele Alessandro would be a total upheaval of her life here. She'd be moving to a culture that she barely knew and would have to learn all the customs and a new language to make it work. Could she give up a life here in the States on the chance that he would make her the priority of his? Shaking her head, she knew she'd probably never have to answer that question. Gabe would stop calling in a few days and go back to his life working fifteen-hour days and missing his childhood sweetheart.

It was better that she was done with it all now than letting things progress. Because at this point, the small heart-break was better than leaving her heart in pieces when things didn't work out.

After leaving another message on Aubrey's phone, Gabe hung up, feeling the weight of exhaustion flow through him. He'd gotten a call from his mother just after lunch on Wednesday that Aubrey had taken off, leaving a note of thanks for the family. The blow of it hit him harder than when Nicoletta had told him about her cancer diagnosis.

He'd left the office and raced over to read the note, which said nothing special for him. He knew she'd felt something for him, but he'd been more distant than he should have. The talk he'd had with his father had put everything into perspective for him, though. Nicoletta had been a big part of his past, but he was ready for a future with Aubrey. But leaving without telling him? It felt like a betrayal of trust all over again.

He hadn't left his parents' home since. It was now Thursday evening, and he needed a shower. But the lack of will to move caused him to stay put.

"What do you think you're doing?" His mother's voice

was raised more than usual, making his head turn in surprise.

"What do you mean? I'm sitting here, watching television." He pointed to the flat screen as if that was proof enough that his wandering mind could recall anything that had flashed on the screen in the last several minutes.

His mother moved to stand in front of him, her small stature now intimidating from his spot on the couch. "I've given you enough time to grovel, but it's time you act. This isn't how you solve things, Gabe. If you love Aubrey, you have to get past your fear of being vulnerable and let her know."

Shaking his head, Gabe said, "There's no way she has feelings for me now."

"Then go show her that you still do. You messed up a few times, but you can still redeem yourself. But not by sitting here, feeling sorry for yourself." She paused, setting a hand on her hip. "I've seen how she looks at you, son. She's a keeper in my book."

Without another word, she moved to another room. The silence was only interrupted by the low buzz of a commercial playing.

What could he do? Fly to see her? Would she turn him away?

Those thoughts alone caused him to want to curl up on the couch and just let the wave of sadness pass over him. Like his mother said, he really had two options: work to forget her, or at least take the chance that she'd forgive him and they could talk through their feelings.

Walking into his old room, he brought out several of his more casual clothes he kept there for when he didn't make it home and packed them in a small duffle. After a quick shower, he walked down the hall and to the door.

"I'm taking the jet. Tell Sophia she's in charge until I get back," he called out, slipping out the door before he could see the smug look on his mother's face. He had to act now before he decided to back out completely.

This whole feeling of love was much different than anything he'd felt for Nicoletta, as he didn't really know what love was. His feelings about the memories he and Nicoletta had shared together seemed more like best friends than anything as strong as love. But after thinking through all the support and encouragement Aubrey had given him in the few days they'd spent together, he knew he loved her, that a life without her by his side wasn't a life he wanted to consider.

The one hang-up he still had was the issue of taking her from her family. Would she be okay with that?

She'd have to forgive him first. He shook his head, chuckling softly as he drove to the hangar. At least Aiden had told him Aubrey was at the ranch. Being able to picture the scene before him helped ease his discomfort somewhat. He just needed to get through the next several hours without turning back.

* * *

When he landed back in the Cedar City airport, he made the familiar trek over to the rental car terminal, dialing Aiden in the process.

"I'm here."

A pause caused Gabe to see if the call had been cut off. "Where's here?" Aiden asked.

"Cedar City. I'm going to get a rental car, and then I'll drive to the ranch. Does your sister have a favorite flower? Anything I could take her that might help her to forgive me?" A chill whipped through Gabe's body, and he tugged his coat a bit tighter against the wind.

"Well, she just went into surgery at the hospital there in Cedar. I don't know how long she'll be in there, but you've flown all that way. You may as well head there first."

Blowing out a breath, Gabe said, "Thanks, Aiden." He hung up the phone, not excited about what he would have to do. He'd hoped to see Aubrey before anyone else and work through everything before he had to face the rest of her family.

After getting a car, he looked up the address to the hospital, using the directions feature to navigate the unfamiliar streets.

He pulled up to it several minutes later, finding parking on one of the last rows. Turning off the engine, he waited, trying to gain enough courage to face what he was about to do. He was Gabriele Alessandro, billionaire and CEO of Cristallo, but when it came to his personal feelings, he felt like a child. What would he say?

Knowing he was losing his nerve, he forced open the door and climbed out, walking toward the door of the hospital. There was a desk with a woman sitting behind it.

"Excuse me, I need to find someone who is in surgery right now. Aubrey Pearson?" He'd taken off his gloves and proceeded to wring them in his hands.

The woman pointed to the left. "Our surgical wing is down that hallway and to the right. There will be a nurse's station that can give you more information."

Nodding, Gabe said, "Thank you so much."

Following her directions, he focused on his breathing. He didn't want to be admitted as well, although that could be a funny story later on. He saw the nurse's station and stopped, asking again about Aubrey.

"Are you a relative?" she asked, looking at him with a bored expression.

"No, ma'am. I'm a friend. I just wanted to sit in the

waiting room until she comes out of surgery." Exhaustion pressed down on him, and he calculated when the last time he'd slept was. Nearly two days ago, give or take on account of the time change.

"I'll need to speak with the people on her account. What is your name?"

"Gabe Alessandro."

The woman wrote it down on a sticky note and nodded. "Just one minute. I'll be right back."

Gabe moved to the wall across from the desk, leaning against it heavily. He needed to get some sleep, but this part was why he'd come, why he'd spent hours flying as he'd played through all the scenarios that could happen once he saw Aubrey again.

It felt as though fifteen or twenty minutes ticked by before the woman reappeared, and Gabe wasn't sure he could stand there much longer.

"Her parents said you can come on through. Please take a badge from the basket there and sign in on this sheet." She pointed to a clipboard with several lines already written with names.

Once he'd completed her instructions, she pressed a button to open the large double doors. "Waiting room is a few doors down to the left."

Gabe's feet felt like lead as he focused on moving forward one step at a time. He could do this. He'd negotiated with some of the biggest power people in the world as far as materials and contracts were concerned. He could speak to the parents of the girl he loved.

When he turned and saw the large open space with chairs spread around the walls, he took another deep breath before going to stand before the Pearsons.

"Hello, Mr. and Mrs. Pearson. Thanks for letting me come back here."

Mrs. Pearson glanced up and grinned, setting her magazine on the chair next to her and standing. She pulled him into a hug. The strength of it helped to infuse some into him.

"What a surprise, Gabe. We're grateful you're here. How was your trip?" she asked.

Mr. Pearson stood, shaking Gabe's hand once Mrs. Pearson let go, and then they motioned to a chair next to them as they sat again. Gabe sank into the plush chair, grateful to sit down finally.

"It was long. I'm a bit tired as I haven't slept in a couple of days. I just, well, I wanted to come and apologize to Aubrey." He searched their faces, wondering if she'd already told them everything. It wouldn't surprise him if she had, but they looked more confused than anything.

"Aubrey didn't tell us much, Gabe. Just that she tore her ACL skiing with you, and then when she made it to New York, she let us know when her flight would be in so we could pick her up in Vegas." Mr. Pearson's eyes narrowed, as if by looking at Gabe like that, he'd be able to discern what had happened.

Running a hand through his hair, Gabe glanced at the ground for a moment, wishing Aubrey could be the one in front of him right then. But then again, maybe some practice would be best.

He turned his gaze back to them, letting out a deep breath before he began. "It's really my fault. I messed up, more than once, as my mother pointed out. I'm in love with your daughter, and I didn't do a great job of showing her that last day or two of her time in Italy. I just wanted to tell her I'm sorry, and I hope she'll forgive me."

Gabe bit his lip as he watched the married couple look at each other, seeming to speak with looks rather than words.

"It can't hurt to try, dear. I'm sure she'll be happy to see you here once she gets out of surgery." Mrs. Pearson leaned forward, patting his leg with her hand, a wide grin on her face.

"Do you know how much longer that will be?" Gabe asked, clasping his hands together and digging his nails in to keep himself awake.

"I'd say another hour or two. Why don't you sit back and rest a bit? We'll wake you when she's coherent."

Gabe nodded. He leaned his back against the chair, sure he wouldn't be able to rest when such a big moment was still to be played out before him. But within a few minutes, the heaviness of his lids took over, and he was sound asleep.

It was hard for Aubrey to wake up. Every part of her body felt so heavy, and her brain was still in a fog. She could hear the beeps of the monitors nearby and familiar voices, but she couldn't get her eyelids to open.

After relaxing for several moments, she was able to open her eyes a little bit, but it took a few blinks to bring things into focus. A nurse stood over her, taking her vitals.

"Surgery went well. You have some visitors in the waiting room. Would you like me to show them in?"

Aubrey's head felt like lead, and she moaned and tried to smile, hoping the nurse would understand. She'd never had the best reaction to anesthesia, but at least she hadn't started puking already.

A few minutes passed with Aubrey staring at the wall in front of her, feeling the medication slowly wear off. Her tongue no longer felt three inches thick, and she figured she could probably speak.

When the door opened, she saw her mother and father. "Thanks for being here, you guys. I know you have a lot to do at the ranch, but it means a lot that you're here." She looked down at the bedsheets, hoping to control the emotions that had been so close to the surface for the past couple of days.

It had taken everything in her to only give her mother the bare minimum of details, not wanting her to get her hopes up that things would work out between Aubrey and Gabe. But it was still one of Aubrey's hopes, and when he wasn't standing behind them, she tried not to look too disappointed. As much of a fairytale as their story had started out, it looked like it was turning into a regular relationship, the magic all gone from it.

Her mother patted her good leg. "We're just glad the surgery went well. We'll let you rest up for a bit. The nurse said you should be ready to be discharged in another hour or so." She paused, rubbing her lips together as though she was trying to work through something. "There's also someone else here who wants to see you."

"Sadie? Evan? Aiden?" Aubrey asked, somewhat eager now.

Her father coughed and said, "Uh, no. But I think you'll still want to talk to him."

Aubrey searched her mind of who "him" could be if it wasn't her best friend and brothers. Maybe her oldest brother, Darren, and his family. But they had stayed behind so Darren could take care of a business retreat who'd come in for the week. Her sister was at some fitness conference in California, so she knew it wouldn't be her and her new husband.

Her father walked over to the door and opened it, waving to someone out in the hall. Aubrey's stomach twisted in knots, not sure if this was a good surprise or a bad one. When the guy was visible in the doorway, she gasped, surprised to see Gabe standing there.

A mixture of happiness and confusion bubbled in her stomach, and she wasn't quite sure what to say or do.

"What are you doing here?" she finally managed.

Silence descended on the room, and a few seconds later, her parents waved and ducked outside, shutting the door behind them.

Aubrey turned her gaze back to Gabe. He looked like he hadn't slept in days, his usually crisp clothes wrinkled and his hair sticking out in all directions.

He moved a few steps closer to the bed, looking at the chair next to it. "Do you mind if I sit?"

Aubrey narrowed her eyes at him, trying to decide what motive he could have for flying across the world to see her. "Fine." She motioned to the chair and leaned her head back against the pillow, not sure she could look at him for too long before her feelings of anger and disappointment would be swept away.

"How are you feeling?" he asked, his voice tender. He reached forward and took her hand, and even though her first reaction was to yank it out of his grasp, she was a mature adult and could handle a few more minutes of electricity between them.

Aubrey turned her head to look at him and saw a genuine smile on his face. "I just got out of surgery, and I'm on plenty of pain killers right now. So not too bad."

She waited for him to continue the conversation, but he just sat there, looking like his tongue was tied. "What are you really doing here, Gabe? I'm sure your company could use your help, or even your girlfriend's family." The words pricked at her eyes, and she turned so he wouldn't see the moisture forming there.

Gabe squeezed her hand a bit. "What do you mean 'my girlfriend's family'? As far as I'm concerned, you're my girlfriend...if you want to be."

"I heard you talking to your father the night before I left.

You were going to some big event for Nicoletta's charity, and you said she was a big part of your past—"

"You must not have stayed long enough to hear what I said after it, then. No wonder you were so mad at me at breakfast." Gabe shook his head, his smile getting wider as the seconds ticked by. He finally looked up at her. "Aubrey, what I said was Nicoletta was a part of my past, but I want you to be my future. The thing that worried me most about us being in a relationship was the fact that I'd be taking you from your family, from everything you'd ever known, while I'd be a quick ride away from my own."

Aubrey realized she'd been holding her breath for several seconds, and as she let it out finally, every part of her tingled with excitement. She wasn't sure what to say as her slow-moving brain was still processing everything she'd heard.

Gabe continued, his eyes filling with tears and his voice choked with emotion. "I know, I messed up. Too many times to count. But I haven't dated anyone seriously since Nicoletta, haven't thought about love or relationships in so long that I was pretty sure I was going to screw things up."

He leaned forward and brushed his thumb across her cheek. "I love you, Aubrey Pearson, and I was an idiot to let you leave, to not talk about this before. I'm not sure how a long-distance relationship works or even if you want that, but I'm willing to give it everything I've got."

As much as she loved hearing the words, the memory of the night they were supposed to go out for dinner and him standing her up wouldn't stop bugging her. "What about work?"

"I was going over applications to hire more people to lighten my workload. I just need to interview and hire them and I will be working normal hours." He sighed. "I just hope you can forgive me and give me another chance."

She shook her head, trying to get the drugs to wear off faster. "Wait, did you say you love me?"

The half-smile she loved so much appeared on his face, and he said, "I did. I love you, Aubrey. I know I haven't shown it all that well, but I do."

Aubrey felt the emotions well up, and tears spilled down her face. "I love you too, Gabe. We've both had our moments, but I kept hoping it would work out between us, that we'd find a way to be together."

Gabe's expression looked like he'd hit the ceiling if he didn't contain his excitement. "You'd be okay dating a guy who lives across the ocean?"

Aubrey reached out both arms and wrapped them around Gabe's neck, pulling him closer. Whispering in his ear, she said, "I'd marry you, Gabe Alessandro."

As crazy fast as things had happened, she didn't feel anything but pure happiness.

Gabe pulled back, studying her face for several seconds, and she took in a breath, hoping she hadn't gone over some unseen boundary.

"Really?" he asked, his eyes full of hope.

Aubrey gave him a quick nod, and he leaned in, pressing his lips to hers. Nothing had ever felt more right in her life, and she hoped that together they would have the life she'd always dreamed of.

They broke apart, their foreheads still touching as they took in deep breaths.

Aubrey grinned and said, "We should probably tell my parents to head home. I've got my own Italian White Knight to get me there."

CHAPTER 30

Gabe felt like a teenage boy who had just asked out his first girlfriend as they drove back to Aubrey's parents' home in Aspen Hollow. He couldn't remember a time when he was so happy. He had hoped for the best, but when she'd said she would marry him, he'd been blown away. He still felt like he was in a dream.

He jumped out and helped her out of the car, steadying her crutches while she slid out of the passenger seat. Even in a pair of sweats and a sweatshirt, she was the most beautiful girl he'd ever seen. He just wished he could go back and redo those last few days when she was in Venice with him so they wouldn't have that mark on their relationship. He would do better from this point on. She made him want to be a better man, one who would always put her first and be there for her.

Aubrey moved with small steps on the crutches, and Gabe wasn't sure how to help exactly, only putting his hand on the small of her back to let her know he was there and would catch her if anything happened.

Instead of moving to the front door, Aubrey shifted over to the porch swing and sat down, lifting a blanket from a basket next to it and spreading it out.

Gabe wasn't quite sure what to make of it, and when she saw his hesitation, she patted the seat next to her. He took it, and Aubrey laid some of the blanket over him as well before leaning against him, her head fitting just under his neck. They rocked a bit, the smell of the outdoors mixed with her vanilla scent making him smile. It was so peaceful here, and everything seemed to clear his mind.

He sighed. "This place is pretty amazing. It would be hard to leave it."

Aubrey nodded softly, but she sat up enough to look at his face. "I used to think that. That I could never live farther away than a six-hour drive from my family. But when I was in Italy with you, I could picture myself living there too. It just depends on how things work out with a certain someone." She gave him a wry grin and tapped him softly on the chest with her fist.

He stared into her eyes, trying to find the words to say that could sum up what he was feeling inside. Excitement, love.

Instead of saying anything, he moved forward, pressing his lips to hers. After all they'd been through in the past few days, he felt closer to her than he'd ever felt with anyone. It seemed impossible to love someone so strongly in such a short amount of time. But he couldn't deny it.

A tingle shot through his lips as he deepened the kiss, and he wrapped his arms around Aubrey, bringing her in closer. After a bit, they pulled back and smiled at one another. He put his forehead against hers, his chest rising and falling at a rapid pace.

"I love you, Aubrey Pearson. We're going to make this relationship last. I'll do whatever it takes."

He leaned in for another kiss, knowing his life would never be the same. And he was okay with that.

ACKNOWLEDGMENTS

Thank you so much for reading this book! I hope you enjoyed it and make sure to leave a review!

You, the reader, are the one I think about as I work through these novels and thank you for continuing to support me. And thank you for being patient as I've been working to grow a baby for the last few months and haven't felt up to writing.

Thank you, Max, for taking the kids every Thursday so I can pour my heart out on the page. I'm a better mother and a more sane wife when I have those small breaks.

Julie L. Spencer, Elizabeth McCay, Shannon Symonds and Deborah Goodman. Some of the best and funnest romance people I could associate with. I love our Thursday night chats and the late hours talking about whatever is going on in our lives. The long Facebook threads and the fun laughter as we work through our bad first drafts down to the final edits.

To Christina Schrunk for her patience in working with me on these books. Her ideas and insight help to spark those last final puzzle pieces to help the book come together and I am so grateful for her.

To Krista Burdine for proofreading this book. She keeps me sane so I don't have to reread the book 100 times before publishing to hopefully get all of the errors out.

To Blue Valley Author Services, AKA Victorine Lieske and her awesome sister for making the cover. Especially for the last minute change of the guys eyes.

If you want news on when the next book comes out or my progress on the series, make sure to subscribe to the list so you don't miss anything.

We are grateful for readers like you and can't wait for you to enjoy the next book!

It had been six months since Aubrey's surgery, and she had finally been completely cleared to return to all her old activities. She'd transferred her job to the hospital in Aspen Hollow and had been able to do a little more work each week, but she was grateful she'd been able to recover there at least.

Gabe had come to California three times over that time, staying for a week and allowing them to get to know more about one another. Every time he left, she found it harder to say goodbye.

This was her first time back to Italy since the skiing accident, and as the plane landed, her excitement in being there made her want the plane to taxi and arrive at the gate much faster than the plane was moving. Then again, it helped that Gabe had bought her a first-class ticket, making the journey much more enjoyable than it had been the first time she'd flown to Europe.

Once off the plane, she looked around, frowning when she didn't see Gabe. She walked to the baggage claim, trying to calm the panic coursing through her that he could have been in an accident and anger that he might be stuck at the office. He'd done really well at hiring people over the past several months, and he'd sounded optimistic about how it was going, but she just couldn't shake the irritation building inside her.

She grabbed her bag and turned toward the exit doors, seeing someone with her name on a board.

"I'm Aubrey Pearson," she huffed. The words flowed better in Italian than they had every time she'd practiced them, but she hoped she'd be able to speak more fluently soon enough.

Looking up, she grinned when she saw Gabe holding the sign. "I'm so glad you're here. I was worried you were going to be stuck at the office or something."

He wrapped her in a hug and pulled back enough to kiss her on the lips. After several seconds, he pulled back with the widest grin she'd ever seen on his face. "You have no idea how badly I've been wanting to do that again. I'm just so glad you're here."

"Probably as long as I've been dreaming about it," Aubrey said, her lips quirked into a smile.

He grabbed the handle to her large suitcase, holding her hand with his other and leading her out the doors and to a black limo. After loading her luggage, they slid into the limo, and Aubrey cuddled up next to him with his arm around her shoulders.

"I'm just glad to be back here again. This has been the longest six months ever." She sighed, breathing in the clean scent of him, grateful this wasn't a dream.

When they stopped, Aubrey looked out the window, surprised to not see the familiar Alessandro home from her last trip. Instead, they were at the docks. Aubrey turned to look at Gabe. "We're not going to your parents' house?"

He smiled and moved a piece of her hair out of her face. "Later. I've got a little surprise for you first. Dante will get your bags to the house for when we get back."

He helped her into his boat, and they took off over to Venice island. Gabe navigated the boat up next to a dock she wasn't familiar with, and she wondered what was going on.

"This isn't where your apartment is either. What's up, Gabe?"

With a chuckle, he took her hand and helped her onto the dock. "I told you, it's a surprise. Now just enjoy the walk. It's a bit warmer than the last time you were here, and there are some vendors I thought you'd like to walk through."

He interlaced his fingers with hers, and she was surprised by the casual way he was walking. They moved in and out of the crowds of people and over small waterways in between buildings. Aubrey realized how much she'd missed this place, the beautiful architecture of the buildings and the buzz of excitement in the air.

As they walked over a bridge, Aubrey turned and came to a stop at the beauty of the scene in front of her. The water was always crystal-clear around Venice, but that combined with the buildings and boats around it made her stop and lean against the railing of the bridge.

"This is amazing. We didn't make it here last time I was in Venice." When she didn't get a response, she turned to see where Gabe had gone, finding him on one knee. Her eyes widened, and she put a hand over her mouth, not believing this was happening.

Gabe took her hand. "Aubrey Marie Pearson, we've been through a lot together in these last few months, and I've never been happier. Will you be my wife?" He pulled out a small velvet box and opened it.

Without breaking her gaze from his face, she pulled him to standing position and kissed him. "Yes. A thousand times yes." He put the ring on her finger, and she kissed him again, still not believing this was completely real.

He pulled back, looking more relieved than ever. "I'm glad you said that. I didn't sleep last night, going through all the scenarios that could have happened. But I also have one more surprise for you." He grabbed something from his back pocket, and when he brought it forward, she saw a bigger velvet box. His hands shook less, but she could still see the excitement and nerves in his face.

He opened the box and there lay a silver chain with a round silver circle, the middle of which was made of glass.

"It's beautiful, Gabe. You didn't have to get me this. I feel bad I don't have something for you."

The corner of his mouth quirked up, and then he looked back at the pendant, his mouth moving but no words coming out. Finally, he spoke.

"Well, I know how important it is for you to have children, to have a family to raise. And I wanted to give you this as a token that I want the same thing. This is a mother's necklace. I've heard it's more of an American thing, but it felt like the right gift to give you. When our children are born, we can put the birthstone in the middle of the pendant."

Tears streaked down her face, and Aubrey pulled Gabe toward her, matching her lips to his. Then she wrapped her arms around him for a long hug, grateful for this small gesture.

"This is the best day of my life," she whispered. "Thank you for this, for both gifts. I will cherish them forever."

Aubrey stood on tiptoe for another short kiss. "Just know that I'm ready when you are."

"So, tomorrow?" he asked, laughing after.

She hit him in the shoulder again. "No. But a couple of weeks to get everyone here should do the trick, don't you think?"

"As long as I'm with you, that's enough for me."

ALSO BY BRITNEY M. MILLS

International Billionaire Series

The Australian Billionaire

The French Billionaire

The British Billionaire

The Vegas Billionaire

The Italian Billionaire

Love Austen Series

Love, Austen

Austen, Party of Two

Austen Unscripted

Matched, Austen

If you liked this book or any of the books in the series, please leave a review. It totally makes my day and helps other readers see them.

Subscribe to the newsletter to get updates on books coming out, cover reveals and the opportunity for giveaways!

Britney Mills was born in Utah but parts of her heart lie in Boston, Washington D.C. and Germany. Her love of writing began with the third grade book her teacher assigned her to write and she spent hours hidden behind her mother's couch writing pages and pages about knights and castles. Now she writes about romance. Go figure.

When she's not mothering her four small children, writing or reading, she's probably out playing a sport, going on a hike, or binge watching a murder mystery series. The way to her heart is through homemade chocolate chip cookies and five minutes peace.

www.ingramcontent.com/pod-product-compliance
Lightning Source LLC
Chambersburg PA
CBHW030754200726
48288CB00004B/1176